EMMA'S TRIAL OF LOVE

BY P.J. HICK

ISBN: 13:978-0-578-49805-8

EMMA'S TRIAL OF LOVE

BY P.J. HICK

The Terrace Hill Mansion was built by Iowa's first millionaire, Benjamin F. Allen. Upon its completion, Mr. and Mrs. Allen invited their friends to the house on January 29, 1869 to celebrate their fifteenth wedding anniversary. The party was an elaborate affair. Stories were written about the party in the Des Moines newspapers. Much of the details in my story about the party and Mr. Allen are based on these articles.

PROLOGUE

NOW

Where was Emma? The words echoed in Abby Hunter's head as she pushed her laptop computer away from her in disgust. She had spent the last three hours exploring all the popular genealogy sites on the internet in hopes of locating Emma, the oldest daughter of Richard and Eliza Edward. Abby had found many women named Emma Edward but none that had been born in Yorkshire, England in 1850 and traveled to the United State with her father, mother, brothers and sister eight years later and settled in a town called Mount Pleasant, Iowa.

Abby sighed and turn to a notebook where she had jotted down all the places she had looked for Emma. She had been to the State Historical Society of Iowa Research Museum, had dug through census reports, family records and books about the history of Mount Pleasant. She had even taken a trip to the town itself, walking the old cemeteries and poking around in its historical district. She had discovered all the graves of Emma's family members, including her parents, brothers David and Jonah, and sister Grace. She knew from prior research that Emma's brother,

Alfred Edward, had died in the Civil War and was buried in Missouri. But there was not a grave for Emma. Abby suspected that Emma had married, and she searched through decades of Henry county marriage records, but the only thing she could conclude was Emma hadn't married a local man. Where had Emma gone?

Abby was determined to find her. It was a mystery she needed to solve. She wouldn't rest until she did. It had become her obsession, to learn as much as she could about this part of her family tree. Abby had found death records, obituaries, probate records for the other members of Emma's family, but none for her. Where was Emma?

ONE

IN THE BEGINNING...

March 10, 1868

The olive-green Concord stagecoach, pulled by the team of four sorrel horses, raced across the Iowa prairie. The driver occasionally used the whip to keep the horses moving at a steady speed. The Western Stage Company was known for its reliability. When the weather was good, it covered eight miles in an hour.

Most of the winter snow had melted, but the temperature was still cold. Inside the coach, Emma Louise Edward scooted forward as far as she could on the stagecoach's ox-hide seat and stretched her neck and head as far as they would go out the door's window. She stared into the distance to try and catch a glimpse of her destination. Emma had been traveling for two days, and she was tired, dirty and cold. They had to be almost there. She squinted her eyes and cocked her head to one side to see better. Hope came to her soul as a row of tiny buildings began to appear. She smiled in glee.

Just then the coach's wheel hit an uneven spot in the road,

bouncing her out of her seat. Emma felt herself falling backwards. She struggled to remain upright, but it was no use, and she landed with a thud on the lap of the man next to her. She heard him let out a grunt. Emma looked into his startled brown eyes. She was suddenly aware of his strong form beneath her. She had never been so close to an unknown man before.

She sought to right herself. In her haste to leave his lap, she placed one of her small hands on his firm thigh and the other on his knee, causing him more discomfort as she rose, scrambling awkwardly like a newborn foal trying to find his feet for the first time. Tiring of her efforts, the man grabbed Emma around her small waist with his hands and deposited her once again in the seat next to him.

He continued to glare at her. His face was handsome, she decided, if you liked a firm, square jaw, a peak for a nose, bushy eyebrows, and dark brown eyes that seem to look straight through you. He had a youthful appearance and looked about the same age as her oldest brother.

Emma could not find any words to apologize in her disarrayed state. She pulled down her skirt over her knees and petticoats. She tucked her long winter coat around her, hoping it would somehow hide her. She placed her hands in her lap like a proper lady should. He watched her intently and Emma blushed red.

He broke the tension as he said, "I take it, Miss, you have not been to Des Moines before?"

His voice came out warm and a bit amused, which gave her courage to reply.

"I have not, sir, and I just wanted to see what kind of settlement it was."

"I think you will find it to your liking. It's grown in recent years to a population of twelve thousand with many fine trading establishments where a woman can buy most anything she might need, including a new hat."

Emma blushed again as she reached out with her gloved hand to claim her bonnet that had fallen off her head and still rested on his lap. She placed it on her head and tied the ribbons under her chin in a bow.

"I could point some of them out as we pass through town." The corners of his mouth turned up in a slight smile.

Emma nodded. "I would like that." She decided to pretend that nothing had happened, and perhaps he would forget that it had, too. "Do you live in Des Moines, sir?"

"I do. I have lived there for ten years and have watched it grow in population. I find the town very pleasant. The Des Moines and Raccoon Rivers are quite beautiful, and now that the bridges have been built over them, it makes it much easier to get around. You are probably aware that the town is now Iowa's state capital. The government once housed in Iowa City moved here not long ago. There is still some debate on which side of town the Capitol building will be constructed. Either on the east side of the river or the west. However, the legislators' activities make for lively topics of conversation among the townsfolk." He paused a moment, then said, "However, I'm quite perplexed that a young lady of your age should be traveling alone. Stagecoach traveling can be dangerous and difficult at this time of year."

Emma sat up straight in her seat. His words offended her. People often thought her younger than she was because of her short stature, round face and thick, curly, brown hair that always escaped from the bun she tied at the base of her neck.

"I'm eighteen," she said. "I am not a child."

The sharp, loud tone of her voice caused the man to draw back in his seat. Emma was surprised at this action. His stocky body and reserved manner had impressed her. She had believed he would fear no man.

"And my father accompanied me on my trip until the last stop when you got on the stage. He had business to conduct in that town. He felt I would be safe until I arrived and met my cousin in Des Moines." She stuck her nose in the air, and her face had gone rigid with displeasure.

"I beg your pardon, Miss. I didn't mean to upset you. I was just concerned for your safety. Look." He pointed out the stage's door. "We have arrived." The speed of the coach had decreased, and the horses were now moving at a slow trot. They stopped for a moment while the driver paid the toll to cross the bridge over the river. They moved forward again. Wood and brick buildings of the Des Moines business district appeared. They passed wagons, horses, and many people walking in the street.

Emma turned to look with interest at the surroundings. For a moment she was mesmerized by what she saw. Des Moines was a much larger town than Mount Pleasant, Iowa, where she was from. They sat quietly taking in the sight.

"Over there," the man pointed with his hand, "is J.M Clouston Fancy & Staple Dry Goods shop. The perfect place to buy readymade clothing, watches and bonnets." He winked at her. "And if you can't find something there, W.W. Moore's City Emporium has many fine things as well. You must also visit Bush's Drugstore. They have a new soda water apparatus. Everyone has been talking about it."

"I'll have to take a stroll when I'm here and make the rounds to the stores you have mentioned." Emma was warming up again to the man. She wondered if he was married and about his life. She was curious about him but was too timid to ask such personal questions.

They pulled up to the Everett House located on Court Avenue and Walnut Street. The coach came to a stop. The Everett House was a fine hotel where a traveler could rent a room for a dollar, and that price included a meal. It also served as the Western Stagecoach station for departures and arrivals.

The man rose and quickly opened the stagecoach's door and disappeared outside. A moment later he extended his hand to her. She took it and stepped out the door of the coach. Before she could step down to the ground, he grabbed her by the waist and pulled her close, then placed her gently on the earth. For the second time that day she felt the warmth of his body against hers. She looked into his eyes and he into hers. A feeling she did not recognize rose inside her. She could not catch her breath and knew not what to do. She had never felt this way before. She stood frozen in his arms.

TWO

ROBERT

"Emma." A familiar male voice called her name.

Emma stepped back quickly and the man that held her did too. He dropped his hands from her waist in a rush. They turned in unison toward the voice.

"I see you have met Robert Harding. I hope he hasn't filled your head with nonsense."

Emma looked at the man beside her, then at the man with the deep, loud voice that had addressed her. He was her cousin's husband, Charles Cooper. Confusion showed in her eyes.

"Nice conversing with you, Miss, during our travels," the man named Robert said. "I hope you enjoy your stay here."

He tipped his hat at Charles and walked quickly down the street. Emma watched his tall figure vanish around the corner of the hotel. She wondered if she would ever see him again, and she found it strange that she cared.

"Best to stay away from that one," Charles growled. "He's a peculiar one."

Charles picked up her traveling case that the stagecoach

driver had thrown down. He hooked his other hand around Emma's elbow and urged her to move down the street.

"Mary can't wait to see you. She will be worried about us, since the stage was an hour late. We'd better hurry."

Emma stumbled beside him. It took her several steps to regain her balance and to match his long stride. She half ran beside him. Charles was a tall, slim man. His long legs stretched out before him in an easy gait, but Emma, a foot shorter than he, found it difficult to keep up.

Charles, at age thirty-two, was an attorney of some importance in town and was used to being obeyed without question. Emma found him to be stern and serious the few times she had met him and considered him an odd match for her amiable cousin. They stopped at his wagon and he hauled her up onto the seat. He then took the reins attached to his gray carriage horse and urged the animal through the town.

They travelled north and soon left behind the business section of Des Moines. They entered into a residential area with wood and brick houses. Some were small dwellings of poor quality, while others were two stories high and of some substance. They also passed some land where no houses stood.

The March wind blew through the barren trees, shaking the few brown leaves that clung to their branches. The January and February snows had melted away some weeks' prior, leaving the dirt road hard and firm beneath their wagon. Yet the temperature was brisk, and Emma felt the cold even with her multiple layers of clothing and heavy winter coat. The sun, hidden behind the clouds, added little warmth to the day.

Although her cousin's home was a short way from the stagecoach station, it seemed like a thousand miles in the company of Charles. He appeared to be cross with her, and she knew not why. He said barely a word to her on their way.

"That's Mrs. Bishop's house. She's the midwife," he said as they passed a small, brick two-story house with a wide porch and a pitched roof. "You may have need of her services when Mary's time comes. Be sure you remember where she lives. I may not be around to fetch her."

Emma nodded in reply and memorized the unremarkable house in her mind. A short time later, they stopped in front of a two-story picturesque, white, Gothic-style house, with a gabled roof over the front door and large glass windows on each side of the entranceway. She departed the wagon and marched up to the oak door. She pushed it open.

"Emma." A sweet, singing voice filled the air. "Is that you?"

"It is," Emma said as she entered the house. She then walked left into the front parlor where her cousin sat on a cloth-covered sofa. The room was of nice size, painted white, and had lace curtains on the windows. She noticed a painted portrait of Charles above the fireplace mantel. Also in the room were several navy cloth-covered chairs with round backs. On a small wooden table sat a kerosene lamp that burned brightly. Decorated on the walls and shelves were souvenirs from the couple's many travels. She walked over the dark-patterned carpet to where Mary sat and hugged her.

"My goodness, you have swollen up like a pumpkin."

Mary reached down and rubbed her hand over her huge stomach. "I have. The baby will come any time now. I'm very glad you were able to come and help me."

Mary glowed. Being with child seemed to agree with her. Emma had never seen a baby born. She knew her role was not to help with the birthing but to keep house and entertain her cousin's four-year-old son, who just at that moment peeked around the corner of the sofa.

Emma reached out her hand and touched the boy's blonde hair. Jack wiggled out of her reach and shied away.

"Jack, that's Emma. There is no need to be afraid. She's here to care for you." Jack, who resembled his mother with his fair skin and light hair, regarded Emma with concern. His blue eyes opened up wide with suspicion. His mouth puckered up as if he might cry.

Charles had placed Emma's traveling bag on the floor and walked to his son and picked him up in his arms.

"He takes a while to feel comfortable with people he doesn't know." Jack wrapped his arms around his father's neck and buried his face against his chest. "But once he decides you're no threat, you will become his best friend." He turned to address his wife. "Emma met our next door neighbor, Mr. Harding."

"She did?" Mary glanced at Emma in surprise.

"He rode the stagecoach with her."

"He's your neighbor?" Emma asked.

"Indeed he is. He lives in the house next door to us. You rode past it on the way here. He bought the Smith's house a year ago. I really liked Nellie Smith. She was one of my dearest friends. I miss her lively conversation." Mary frowned, her face sad. "We did a lot of things together. However, her husband was an adventurer. He could not stay in one place long. He decided to move out west. It was one of the saddest day in my life when they left." Mary sighed. Charles touched his wife's shoulder in a comforting manner.

"Then Robert moved in." She shook her head in disapproval.

Mary continued, "He is a strange one. He never speaks a word to us. He looks gloomy all the time and sometimes we hear screams coming from his house. I found him, last summer, roaming his gardens in the dead of night. I thought he was an intruder. He scared me to death. It's best you stay away from him."

"I agree," Charles said.

Emma rolled this information around in her head. Try as she might, she could not reconcile her cousin's descriptions with the man she had met on the stage.

"He seemed pleasant enough when we spoke."

Mary studied her cousin and saw the gleam of interest in her eyes that an only a man can bring. Mary knew her cousin was inexperienced when it came to men and any little attention shown by one might turn her head. Eight years older than Emma, Mary had seen more of the world and knew some men were not to be trusted.

"He's too old for you and odd. Don't get any ideas."

"How old is he?"

"Close to my age, twenty-eight or thirty I imagine. Old enough to have been in the Civil War," Charles said. His voice told Emma not to continue on this subject.

Emma walked away from the group and sat down on a chair. She took off her bonnet and gloves. She unbuttoned her coat. Charles came over to her and helped her out of it. He placed her coat on the back of the chair.

For the first time in two days, Emma was warm. She felt suddenly tired. The stagecoach ride had been bumpy and rough.

As if she had read Emma's thoughts, Mary asked, "How was your trip?"

"Cold. We left Iowa City at seven a.m. and father, thank

goodness, had foresight enough to rent a hot soapstone and a buffalo robe from the stagecoach company. These things kept us warm for a while, but the March temperatures still chilled me. I was glad for the hot beverages at each relay station. The sleeping accommodations last night were not the best and I found the bed hard. However, the food at the inn was good. Then this morning we ran into a mud hole. Father and the other male passengers had to help the driver pry the back of the stagecoach's wheels out of the hole with a fence rail. It delayed us for a while. We were forced to walk for a half mile and my skirt became caked with mud." She lifted her skirt to show the others. "I have to admit I am glad the trip is over and I don't have to repeat the experience anytime soon."

"You poor dear," Mary said. "Perhaps you should try the train next time."

"Father said the stage is cheaper."

"Talking of your parents, how are your father and your mother doing?"

Emma thought a moment about the question and didn't know quite how to answer it. How was anyone after two of their children had died? Alfred in the Civil War three years ago, and Grace two months ago from La Grippa, the flu. Her death had been unexpected and sudden.

Emma felt her sister's loss the most. Alfred had been gone to war for so long that when he died, it felt like he was just still gone and someday would return. But Grace, well Grace had been the sunshine in their house, always laughing and finding some prank to play on them. At thirteen, she had not yet grown into adult ways. She would always tell you what was on her mind, and she had not learned the habit of hiding from the truth. Emma had shared a room with Grace, and every time she looked at Grace's bed, the ache of emptiness returned.

She felt like a prisoner in her home with two other inmates. They found nothing to talk about, and she felt like she might go mad. Bleak was their existence. She needed to find a way out of there and make a life for herself. She intended to explore Des Moines to see what opportunities might be here for her.

"Father is angry at everybody and will not attend church services. He understands not why Gracie had to die. He is short-tempered and speaks to us in a loud, irate voice. He is easily provoked. I try to stay out of his way. Mother is heartbroken. I have caught her crying in her room many times with her Bible in her hands. She tries to find some comfort in the words. She told me several times she now knows how the mother of Jesus felt and seeks strength from her example. She has lost a lot of weight. You would barely recognize her. She tries to put on a brave face, but you can tell it's just a front. They barely talk to each other. I think with me gone and out of the house, they might console each other and perhaps find some common ground. Your request for me to come came at a very good time for all of our household."

The impact of her words showed on Mary's and Charles' faces. The joy of Emma coming had suddenly turned sour.

"It's a shame what has happened," Mary said. "I can't imagine losing a child."

"Nor I," echoed Charles as he bent and placed his son on the floor. The little boy looked at Emma, then darted out of the room into the back parlor, which was the room where the family spent most of their time together. The front parlor was kept clean and tidy to entertain their guests. It was a beautiful room. Emma noted how quick the boy was and knew her job to keep tabs on him in the weeks to come would not be an easy one.

"Perhaps you would like to freshen up from your journey. Charles prepared the upstairs bedroom for you. There is a pitcher of water in the room for you to wash yourself. We are all living on the first floor at the present. I can't manage the stairs. If you get too cold at night, let me know and we will make other arrangements."

Charles picked up her bag and led her up the stairs to a small, clean room with a four-poster bed, a bureau, and a small table.

"My mother plucked the breasts of all her chickens to make this feather bed mattress. She gave it to us as a wedding present. I find it too soft for my taste, but hopefully it will suit you."

"I'm sure it will." Emma looked approvingly at the bed and was glad that its length was long. She was not into the fashion of sleeping in a sitting position, a position that was supposed to promote good health. She thought that the practice was odd when her friends had told her about it.

Charles placed her bag near the bed. He then left Emma and returned downstairs.

Emma went to the pitcher on the table and poured water into the bowl. She took the white cloth next to it and dipped it into the water. She washed her face and hands. She then took off her shoes, socks and her traveling attire. She opened her traveling bag, pulled out a fresh blouse and skirt, and changed her clothes. She would have to ask her cousin where to wash her dirty clothes. Feeling much cleaner, she went to the window and looked out at the view and the brick house next door, Robert's house. It, too, was two stories. It had an imposing brick tower that rose upward in the middle of the flat roof. This small square room was positioned high above the entranceway. She imagined Robert there looking out, or, remembering her cousin's story about hearing screams, perhaps his crazy relative lived there.

She was much more curious about the man now than when she got off the stagecoach. She saw a movement far below her. She gasped when she recognized the figure as Robert.

Robert stopped before he entered his house. He lingered there, not moving. The fading light of day outlined his body. Emma watched him intently. What was he doing? Then he lifted his head. He looked up and for a moment she thought he recognized her in the window. She pulled back behind the shades in hopes that he had not seen her. She felt foolish, her heart beating rapidly in her chest. Had she done something wrong?

She eased herself down on the bed and felt herself sink into the middle of the mattress. Its sides raised up around her like an embrace. The mattress was indeed soft. She closed her eyes. She lay thinking about Robert's deep brown eyes and the way his lips curled up when he was amused and what that did to her. She felt his arms around her for that one brief moment.

It had been a long time since she had felt something else other than sadness and emptiness. Was it wrong to steal a bit of happiness from a man she didn't know? Could their meeting be a tiny gift to ease her sorrow for a moment, or was he a temptation from the devil to lead her astray?

Stay away from him. Her cousin's voice echoed in her head as she drifted to sleep for a short nap.

THREE

NIGHTMARES

Robert was tired. It had been a long day. After getting off the stage he had to report to Mr. Benjamin Allen, a well-respected banker who lived in Des Moines. Robert was part of the group of craftsmen that was building Allen's house. And what a house it was. The house was a twenty-room mansion designed by the Chicago architect, William Boyington. The Daily State Register newspaper called it "Americanized Italian" style with a mansard roof.

The house was brick with touches of cut stone and white painted wood trim. It had a ninety-foot high tower that made the one on his house look small. The house sat on a bluff overlooking the Raccoon River Valley some distance west of Des Moines. It was surrounded by twenty-nine acres of beautiful prairie land.

Construction had started on the house in 1867 and it was near completion. He was happy to report to Mr. Allen that the gardener's house was finished and with any luck, the big house would be done by this summer.

The man was spending a lot of money on the house, more than Robert could imagine. The workmen had talked among themselves, adding up the cost of materials and the expensive extra items that Allen had ordered. A sum of two hundred fifty thousand dollars for the house construction had made the rounds. Robert thought the amount quite high since his dwelling cost a mere twelve hundred dollars. But his house was nothing like the mansion.

Robert stopped in the entryway before walking inside. He opened the door and reached for the kerosene lamp he kept on a table. His house was dark as a tomb and just as cold. He lit his lamp and walked to the fireplace in the parlor. He placed a log in it and started a fire. He sat in the chair near the flames and let his mind wander. He knew this was not a good idea for his mind. Often times it brought up memories he did not want to remember.

This time his mind went back a couple of weeks when he was in the Gottscha's Saloon. He had gone there with several other workmen from the Allens' house. They had enjoyed a beer, but he did not order one. He instead had enjoyed their company. Robert had seen what too much drink could do to a man, and he wanted no part it. The saloon was full of men debating the day's affairs.

A fight broke out. One of the men under the influence of liquor flashed a knife. Robert had tried to disarm the man by grabbing him by the arm. But the man escaped and stabbed William Carson in the breast and stomach. Blood went everywhere and for a moment, Robert lost all sense of time. He heard again the cries of other wounded men. He stumbled out the door in agony, trying to get away. He could barely breathe and his head was foggy. He cried out, but his voice was muffled by the fight still raging. Somehow he had sense enough to run and alert the doctors. He did not return to the saloon.

He read in the newspaper a couple of days later that Dr. Grimes and Dr. Brown had arrived at the Saloon. They came to

Mr. Carson and another injured man's assistance. They stretched the injured men out on a couple of the beer tables and tended to their gaping wounds. Two other men, Mark Herry and Nic Donnell, were later arrested by the police. There was no word whether or not Carson had lived. Robert had met Mr. Carson that night and had a lively conversation with him. Carson seemed a pleasant sort and had come to Iowa from Germany.

This incident had caused Robert to sleep poorly and when he did sleep, nightmares came. He saw blood everywhere and bodies of men without limbs. He awoke in a cold sweat. He had gotten up and paced his house, afraid to return to his bed.

The next day at work had been hard. His concentration had been bad, and he jumped at the tiniest noise. He kept looking over his shoulder to make sure no one approached him from the rear. He had an anxious feeling in his gut that would not go away. His thoughts ran wild. He willed these intrusive thoughts to leave him alone. He had chased them away by sheer will and the hard work of his job. He tried to find pleasure in watching beauty come from his labor, but that too eluded him. He labored long and hard those weeks until his body ached from his efforts. He was the first to arrive in the morning and the last to leave. His body finally grew tired by his work activity and overcame the nightmares that plagued him. He fell into a dead, exhausted sleep and slept through the night.

Des Moines was a peaceful town and the incident at the bar was a rare occurrence. The townsfolk, however, were all talking about it. Some believed Des Moines needed a larger police force. At the moment, only one man patrolled the streets at night. Robert agreed with them. He decided never to go to a saloon again.

Willfully, he turned his thoughts to something more pleasant.

He settled on Emma. He did not know what her last name was. She had been a surprise. He thought her a young girl in her bulky winter coat and bonnet, her form hidden from his view, but he was glad she was of age. It made his attraction to her more proper. He liked the way she had stood up for herself when he had mistaken her for a girl. He liked a woman with spirit, and Emma and showed him she was one of those. He had watched her for most of the trip and had taken in her fine features. She had dainty hands, a small nose and large round eyes. She reminded him of a well-bred horse with good conformation.

He wondered if he would have an opportunity to meet her again. If he had been on good terms with his neighbors, the Coopers, he would have stopped by and spoken to her. But Charles didn't like him. Charles was a highly-educated man from a well-to-do family. Robert was not in his class.

The fire soon warmed his house. He watched the logs burn. Their glowing embers reminded him of other fires. He had experienced a lot in his life, and at times he felt very old.

He enjoyed his house. Every man should have a place of his own. A place where he belonged and could put down roots. He was a lucky man and he knew it. He had a roof over his head, food on his table, and had saved enough money to pay his taxes and to see him through a bad time if it should come. He smiled contently into the fire and he was thankful.

But trouble always followed him just like the incident in the bar. No matter how hard he worked and how good he was, trouble came. He had been born under an unlucky star, and he waited anxiously most days to see what would happen next.

FOUR

BABY ARRIVES

Emma placed the last wood block on the small square structure before her. She sat on a chair at a small table in the back parlor.

"Do you like my house, Jack?" she asked the child before her. She had spent most of the morning trying to gain the boy's favor, and it seemed to be working. She had brought a bag of small wood blocks that had belonged to her brothers when they were young. They had spent hours playing with them. Jack eyed the house with interest. He too had been laying blocks on top of one another but had not produced a structure as fine as Emma's. He lifted his hand, then in a swift movement he pushed the house to the ground, scattering the blocks in all directions. He laughed. Emma smirked at him. It was the third time he had destroyed a house built by her.

"Again," he said, smiling at her with pleasure. He then leaped to his feet and jumped onto the red saddle on his brown wooden rocking horse not far from Emma and pretended to ride away. The rocking horse went nowhere except up and down at a rapid pace. He giggled as he rode. Emma wondered what he was thinking. Perhaps he believed himself a soldier that had just torn down an enemy's fort, or perhaps he was an Indian riding to warn his tribe about houses the white men were building on their land.

His mother walked over to Jack and laid a hand on his shoulder, quieting his rocking motion.

"Enough," she said. "Time to take a nap. Help Emma put the blocks away."

Jack reluctantly dismounted his horse. Emma and Jack picked up the blocks. They placed them in the tan canvas bag. Jack clutched the bag in his little hands, not willing to part with his new toys.

"You can take them to your room," Emma said. "Put them somewhere safe, and we will play again tomorrow."

Jack nodded as he followed his mother out of the room. Mary's passage was slow. Her large belly made her waddle in a funny way. Emma reflected on this as she watched the pair disappear. Her plan had worked. Jack was starting to trust her. Her cousin seemed relieved that her son was starting to take a liking to Emma.

It had been hard to gain Jack's confidence. This morning at breakfast in the dining room, he wanted nothing to do with her. He had refused to sit in the chair next to her and preferred instead to sit on his father's lap. He barely looked at her and spoke not a word. At times, he raised the blue check tablecloth and hid his face in it. It had taken almost an hour of her softly talking to the child before he agreed to sit on the floor next to her to see what she had brought in the canvas bag. But once he saw the wood blocks and how they could be stacked to form a building, he had been won over. They had played happily together for some time.

Mary returned to the parlor and lowered herself slowly to the chair next to Emma.

"It is a good thing you came quickly after you received my letter. My mother was to stay with us, but she took ill recently and is recovering. She didn't feel she could assist me. She was afraid she would put me at risk and the new baby, too. I feel the baby will be born soon. I had some pains yesterday, and they are back again today. They are coming more frequently now. I prayed that my child's birth would wait until you arrived. Did Charles point out the midwife's house on your travels?"

"He did."

"Good." Mary breathed heavily. Her huge belly made her lungs work harder. "You told me how your parents are doing. What about you? How are you doing?"

Emma tried not to cry. She had done enough of that.

"Getting by. It is hard when I have nothing to occupy my mind. I have decided that I would like to be useful and earn my own way. I can't live at home forever."

Mary studied her cousin. "That is very forward thinking. Perhaps you have listened to too many of the suffragette ladies' speeches. Do you not want a home and children of your own?"

"I have been to several suffragette meetings, and I do believe that women should have the right to vote. But their ideas have nothing to do with my decision. I'm afraid all the men I knew have either died in the war or have already taken a wife. I was not chosen. I can't just wait around hoping for a change in my situation. Living on my father's farm, I have little chance of meeting a bachelor, and it seems a waste of time to do so. I need to have a purpose. Something worthwhile to do. Somewhere I can help people. I thought I might find some job here in Des Moines. I like children. Perhaps a job as a teacher or a governess. My parents allowed me to take some classes at Iowa Wesleyan College in my home town last fall which helped prepare me to teach."

Mary could feel the despair in her cousin. It was written all over her face.

"I'll see if Charles can ask around town. Perhaps he can find a position for you. But for the next month you are needed here. It will be awhile before I am able to manage on my own."

Emma smiled. She was glad to be here, to be needed.

Mary shifted uneasily on the chair. She groaned. "Oh dear."

"What is it?"

"My water has broken. Help me to my bed, then go for the midwife."

Emma stared at the mess and knew not what to do. She finally rose and put her arm around Mary's shoulder and helped her to her feet. They walked together the short distance through the front parlor to the room across the hall, Mary's bedroom. Emma did what she could to make Mary comfortable on the bed. Emma walked towards the door just as Mary groaned again. Emma stood undecided whether to stay or go.

"Will you be fine while I'm gone?"

Mary waved her hand. "Go," She demanded, her face a bit red and etched with pain. "Get the midwife now!"

Emma rushed to put on her coat and bonnet. Then she flew out the door. Rain greeted her and the wind blew it in her face. She was shocked to realize that while she had been having fun with Jack, a March storm had blown into town. The icy cold raindrops soaked her clothes. The dirt road was already deep in mud, slowing her passage. But she was not going to be sidetracked. She ran with determination the way Charles and she had come the day before, her boots making tracks in mud.

She looked at the houses to her right as she went. How far was it to the midwife's house? The distance seemed longer now that she was on foot instead of in the wagon. The rain clouded her vision. She passed several dwellings, but they did not look like the one she was hunting. She walked on, but she was becoming confused. It seemed like she had gone too far. Or had she not gone far enough? Her thoughts turned to her cousin and she wondered if Mary was in much pain.

Then she saw the two-story brick house with a decorated entrance and cast window caps. This must be it. Or was it? The house not far from it looked much the same. It too was a two-story brick structure with a mansard roof, oval attic windows and a porch. She came to a halt and stared at the houses. Rain pelted her face, and she had forgotten to put on her gloves. Her hands felt like ice as the cold wetness soaked them again.

Help me oh heavenly Father to find the midwife. I don't even know if I have come to the right place.

She said the prayer in a whisper, and no sooner had she finished than she heard a voice call her name.

"Emma, what are you doing out in the rain?"

The lightning pierced the sky. Thunder followed. Emma was frozen in her tracks. Her heart raced. Could God really be speaking to her? Was she losing her mind? Hadn't one of God's prophets gone up to a mountain and after the rainstorm, heard God's voice? Elijah. Yes, that was the prophet's name.

The deep male voice spoke her name again. It came from behind her. She turned around, trembling from head to toe in a daze. She found not God or an angel, but Robert Harding sitting on a bay horse that was standing on the dirt road not far from her. A black cloak covered his body from his shoulders to his toes. Thunder roared and the horse snorted and jumped under the man. Robert tightened his rein so the horse would not run over Emma. He laid a gloved hand on his mount and gently rubbed its wet, sleek, arched neck.

"Easy fellow."

"It's Mary," Emma shouted over the storm. "She's having her baby and I know not which house belongs to the midwife!"

Robert pointed to the next house, the one with the circled attic window and a porch. "Mrs. Bishop lives there."

Emma nodded and ran toward the small house. She reached the porch. She then looked back and saw Robert looking at her.

"Could you go get Charles? He's not home," she shouted.

Robert turned his horse around and started back the way he had come. He shouted back, "I will." He put his horse into a trot as Emma pounded on the door of the house.

A woman twenty years older than Emma opened the door. Her blue eyes stared at the girl.

"My goodness child, what are you doing out on a day like this?" She pulled Emma into the house's entranceway. "You're as wet as a mother duck. Who are you and how can I help you?"

The woman was as round as a fattened turkey. Her grayish-brown hair, tied up in a bun on the back of her head, accented her plump jowls and smiling red lips. Her friendly demeanor knocked any fear Emma had right out of her.

"I'm Emma Edward, Mary Cooper's cousin. The baby is coming and I came to fetch you."

"Well, her little one picked quite the lovely day to be born. Let me get my coat and bag."

Mrs. Bishop stepped back into the parlor. A few minutes later she returned dressed for the weather. Together they walked into the storm. The heavy downpour suddenly stopped and turned instead into a slow, steady light rain. In the gray-blue sky the dark clouds hung low, casting a haunted feeling over the day. The two women walked briskly down the street.

"Second babies usually come quicker than the first. Was she in much distress when you left?"

"Some," Emma said. "I know nothing about birthing babies and I'm not a good judge of what is to come."

Mrs. Bishop nodded.

The trip back to her cousin's house seemed shorter than the one to fetch the midwife. Soon they were at their destination. When they opened the door they heard Mary yell in pain. Jack, awakening from his sleep, answered back.

"Mother, are you all right?" He ran from his room towards his mother. Emma caught him and picked him up in her arms.

"It's all right Jack," Emma said as she held him close. "Mrs. Bishop is here to help your mother. You will soon have a new baby brother or sister to play with."

Jack struggled in her arms in protest. He was a big burden in Emma's arms and she had to hold him tight or he would escape from her grasp. Emma led the way to Mary's room.

"See, your mother is fine." Jack peeked into the room.

"Thank goodness you came," Mary said to Mrs. Bishop as the woman removed her coat and hat. Mrs. Bishop laid a hand gently on Mary's shoulder.

"It will be over soon enough. How are the pains?"

"They are coming quickly now, one after another."

Mrs. Bishop nodded as Emma left and walked upstairs to her room with Jack in her arms.

"I have another toy for you, Jack."

"I want my mother," muttered the little boy, wiggling in her arms.

"I know," Emma said. "But she has work to do and you must not bother her right now."

Emma's arms began to ache. Jack weighed more than a sack of flour, but she dared not let go. They heard Mary groan again, and Jack struggled harder to be free.

FIVE

FAMILY

Robert Harding unsaddled his horse, named Soldier, in his barn. Robert's thoughts turned to his neighbor. Charles Cooper had been shocked when Robert had arrived at his law office. He had been sitting at his desk reading a law book. A cabinet lined with other law books was positioned behind him. In his gray suit, Charles had looked every inch the lawyer he was. His expression turned to surprise, then to dismay when Robert had told him his reason for coming. The two men had then ridden side by side on their horses to their homes. They spoke not a word to each other. Robert sensed Charles' concern for his wife. There was little that a man could do while his wife gave birth to their children except pace the floor and hope his wife survived the outcome. Some did, some didn't.

Robert had been old enough to remember his youngest sisters' birth. He had sat with his father in his parent's home listening to his mother's moans while she had delivered not one baby, but two. Her groans and whimpers had filled their house with noise for several hours. Robert knew that birthing a child was a difficult task for women, and he had deep respect for their suffering.

The thunder sounded and his horse trembled under his hands. He spoke softly to the animal. The horse had seen battle during the civil war and had barely survived the outcome. Robert had bought the horse from the union army when the animal was thin and could barely stand. Robert had felt the horse deserved a loving home in his final days for the service he had performed for the military.

The horse had surprised him. Robert's tender care had brought the animal back to life, and now the horse was quite the beauty. But the horse still shook and became terrified when the thunder roared. Robert understood his reaction, for the roar of thunder also reminded him of the great cannons that had been fired during the war, and like his horse he wanted nothing more to do with them.

After tending to his horse, Robert walked through his yard to his house. He looked over at the house next to his and wondered what was happening there. Was Charles rejoicing over the birth of a new child or was he crying bitter tears over the loss of his wife? Robert's Uncle John had lost a wife that way, and he had chosen never to marry again. He had raised the son that had caused his heartbreak by himself. It took many years before he could forgive himself for the death of his wife. He had not called the doctor to aid his wife until two days after the birth and by that time it had been too late.

Robert's father and mother, who lived near his uncle, had taken the baby and raised it until it was two years old, then returned the boy to his uncle. His Uncle John by that time had overcome his grief and poured his love into his little boy. Robert envied his cousin who from that day forward always seem to have more than enough of everything, food, clothes and horses.

It had been much different in Robert's family. He slept with his three younger brothers on one bed. He learned never to have seconds at meal time and only take what food he really needed. He was taught to share whatever clothing he had with his brothers, to work hard, never to complain and look after the younger ones. His father's word was the law in the house, and if you disobeyed you might get a whipping with his belt or no supper, which Robert learned was worse than the belt. Nothing was worse than no food in your belly. Yet even with so many people in their household, they somehow had gotten along and had also had some happy times.

Robert opened the door to his house. It was not a fancy home like some of the ones he helped build. He had few pieces of furniture in the rooms, but what he did own was of high quality. The war had changed him when it came to material things. He had learned how little men could live with and still survive. It had made him appreciate the little things in life. He had bought his house with all his savings and a bank loan from Mr. Allen. He had heard that Mr. Allen was generous with his money, having helped many a business and other people reach for their dreams. This had proved to be true.

He had bought his house after he tired of living in rented rooms. He had wanted a place of his own. He could have bought farm land away from Des Moines like many other folks. But after watching his father labor to feed his family on the small plot of land he owned, Robert wanted no part of farming.

Robert, the oldest boy in his family of ten siblings, had helped his father in the fields at planting and harvest time, starting when he was seven years old. It had been hard work. His parents lived in the state of Ohio, and he hadn't seen them for some time. Robert had left Ohio when he was sixteen and moved to Iowa with his sister, Lena, and her husband, George Anderson, in hope of a better life.

Thoughts about his own family made him wonder what kind of family the Coopers were. He pondered this as he entered his home.

❧

Emma cuddled the little baby girl wrapped in the blanket to her heart. She rocked back and forth in the chair to calm the child. The tiny bundle didn't even open her eyes to greet her new relatives. She wiggled instead and punched a tiny fist in the air.

"Ah," Mrs. Bishop said. "Mary did just fine and delivered this little beauty with no problems, she did. Look at all that brown hair. She is quite pretty. Don't you agree, Mr. Cooper?"

"That I do. She will grow up to break many men's hearts." He pulled his young son, Jack, forward until he stood in front of Emma. "Jack meet your new sister, Collette Maria Cooper." The little boy put out his hand to stroke the baby's head. "Touch her gently. That's right. She's part of our family now and we need to protect and care for her. That's what family members do. They help each other through the good and bad times."

That's what families do. Emma repeated the words in her head. She agreed with what Charles had said. The baby kicked its little legs under the blanket, hitting Emma in the chest. The kick, more like a tap, made Emma smile. This newborn child brought out maternal feelings in Emma. This is how all mothers must feel.

Pride in their young and a protectiveness of a new life. This indeed was a woman's purpose. A purpose she would never know.

For a moment a tear formed in her eye as the excitement of this new life turned into self-pity for her station in life. Spinsters like herself often stayed as domestic help for their other family members, taking care of aging parents, offering a helping hand to her aunts and uncles in time of need. Finding a job or purpose of her own was a new vision that only the suffragette woman thought about. Emma had considered this new reasoning, and if marriage was not to happen to her, she was determined to find her own place in this world.

SIX

JACK IS MISSING

Emma settled quite nicely into the Cooper household. She had taken on the duties of cooking and doing laundry for Mary. With a new baby there was always laundry to do, and since Emma loved to cook, the cooking was no chore at all. Being the oldest girl in her family, her mother had taught her how to cook over an open fire in the fireplace and just recently with a wood-burning stove.

Mary had a stove as well. Emma was experimenting with it with her favorite recipes that she knew by heart. How long to bake something differed when using the stove. Wood was put on one side of the stove and its heat warmed the chamber next to it and the grill above. You cooked meals in the heated chamber.

Mary confided to Emma that she was not a good cook and had recently purchased a cookbook from one of the stores in town to help her. Emma had read through the book and was using one of its recipes to make biscuits. The recipe was much like one her mother had taught her as a child. The ingredients in the recipe were few: two quarts of flour, one pint of sour milk, one half-cup of lard or butter, two teaspoons of saleratus and a pinch of salt.

Emma was kneading the dough when Mary walked into the kitchen with the baby in her arms. Jack trailed behind her.

"Charles came home early for a change. He wonders when dinner will be ready."

Emma had found out that the household ran on Charles' schedule. Charles was up most mornings before the sun and expected some sort of breakfast to be ready. If he was late from work, dinner was kept warm until he arrived. If he came home in a bad mood, Jack was kept out of his way and was told to play in his room. If he wanted to talk about the events of the day, Mary and Emma sat in their chairs, hanging on every word he said.

Charles was a good storyteller and had a smart mind for small details that made his conversations interesting. Emma thought of him as an actor and believed he could have done well in the theater. He liked center stage and did not like to be interrupted when talking, not even when the baby cried and demanded attention.

As if Collette knew Emma's thoughts, she let out a cry that filled the kitchen. She then continued to cry as Mary rocked her and tried to sooth her. Jack touched his mother's arms and tried to pat the baby.

"It will be alright," he said to the newborn infant. "We'll take you back where you came from. You don't need to be afraid."

Emma and Mary tried not to laugh at Jack's statement.

"She belongs to us now, son. There is no taking her back," Mary said. "There, there, Collette, is this better?" Mary placed the baby's head on her shoulder and rubbed her back. The little girl stopped her wailing.

"Supper will be done in twenty minutes. I need just to bake the biscuits. The table is set and the stewed beef steak is already done. I also made a fine pudding for after the meal. Charles can have what is left of it for breakfast tomorrow."

Emma divided up the dough and rolled the pieces into small balls. She placed them on a baking pan, then into the oven.

Mary smiled and turned to leave.

"You're a blessing, Emma Edward, and I don't know what I would have done without you these past two weeks."

Mary had suffered some from childbirth and was now just getting back on her feet. She turned to leave to go sit in the front parlor. Jack darted out of the kitchen ahead of her.

Emma looked out the kitchen window at Robert's house. It was dark and not a soul moved within it. If she didn't know better, she would have thought the house abandoned. The fact was she had not seen Robert since the day the baby was born. She had often walked outside the past two weeks with young Jack, who was always full of energy and needed to run and play. While Jack played in the yard, Emma sat on the porch and stared at the brick house next door. She now knew which window was slightly cracked and how many steps it was to the entrance door. She enjoyed looking at the fine decoration along its roof. She tried to imagine what the inside looked like. Was it simple and plain like her parents' house or fancy with many fine things like her cousin's?

Directly behind Robert's house was a small fruit orchard with many trees, and beyond that a small shed which housed his horse. The trees were bare of leaves and fruit and the grass brown from the winter. But she could tell they had been trimmed in the fall. Robert kept the garden and his house well-tended. There were no extra items or broken tree branches scattered around the house. Nor was the house run down like some she had seen in Des Moines. This, in Emma's opinion, made him a good neighbor.

There was little else she could conclude or learn about the man from his property. She did wonder what kept Robert out late at night. When she looked at his house from her bedroom window before retiring for the night, she saw no lights. What did he do for a living? He must have some means to afford such a house. Was he a storekeeper, a baker, a newspaper editor or a teacher?

She had heard no screams from the property, and the only noise the house made was a slight banging from a loose board. She had hoped to stumble into Robert so she could thank him for helping her. But Robert was never around, or if he was, he was good at hiding from her. She, however, was still curious about the man. Sometimes at night before she fell asleep, she would make up stories about him in her head.

Emma finished dinner and went to put it on the dining room table. She liked having a dining room. It was separate from the parlors and kitchen. Her parents' house was smaller than Mary's and they ate on a table in the kitchen. Mary's dining room was cheerful with patterned sky-blue wallpaper on the walls and a matching checkered blue tablecloth. Emma had set the table with china dishes and placed the food on the table. She called the others to come into the room. Mary arrived first and put the baby in a cradle nearby. Charles followed after her, but Jack did not appear. Charles called his son's name impatiently, but the boy did not come.

"I will fetch him," Emma said. She walked through the rooms. She discovered that Jack was not in the downstairs. Emma went upstairs to his bedroom. She became worried when his room was empty. She searched the upstairs rooms and found him missing. She returned to the dining room in hope he had appeared, but he was not there.

"I can't find him," she proclaimed.

Charles jumped from his chair and repeated the search of the rooms with no success.

"Look Emma," he said, "the front door is ajar. Perhaps he is outside."

"Where has he gone?" Mary cried.

"I don't know, but I will find him," her husband said.

Dinner was forgotten as Charles and Emma quickly put on their outer coats and went outside. Mary followed and stood at the door, calling her son's name.

It was still early spring and the sun was fading from the sky, causing it to turn gold and red. Darkness soon followed and eerie shadows formed on the yard. The trees were darker, still hiding anything that might be near them. Charles charged around the yard like a raging bull, bellowing in fear. Emma felt scared. Where could the four-year-old boy have gone?

They searched everywhere around the house and down the street. Minutes turned into an hour. The night grew darker.

Suddenly there was movement from the house next door. A tall, dark form strolled from the back of the house and came towards them. The darkness hid his face and features. Then the moon shone on him briefly and his face looked like a ghost. The form was large and looked threatening in the dark. Emma knew it could not be Jack. She feared for Jack's safety. Her breath caught in her chest. Charles saw the form and ran toward it, and Emma did too.

"Papa," cried a small voice. "Help me."

"Stop, what are you doing?" Charles screamed at the form. When Charles and Emma reached the figure, Emma saw it was Robert and in his arms, young Jack was crying. Charles, in one swift motion, tore his son from Robert's arms. Robert let loose of the boy.

"How dare you take my son? What have you done to him?"

Robert snapped back at Charles, "I have done nothing. I found him alone and shivering in the cold."

"An unlikely story if I ever heard one. You took him from our yard. Don't ever touch one of my children again." Charles turned and dashed back to the house. He then put Jack in Mary's waiting arms.

Emma stood in the dark, quite perplexed at what had just happened. She stared at the astonished Robert. She could barely make out the outline of his face. Emma, unlike Charles, did not think his story untrue. They stood across from each other for a moment or two.

"The boy was crying. I picked him up. I meant no harm," he said in a tired voice.

Emma said, "I thank you once more for coming to our aid. I will talk to Charles. It's just that he was very frightened."

Robert nodded his head. "As well he should be."

"Emma," Mary called. "Where are you?"

"I'm coming." Emma swiftly walked toward the house, leaving Robert in the shadows.

By the time Emma had gotten back to the house, Jack had stop his crying, although his eyes were red. He was sitting on Mary's lap at the dining room table. Charles was kneeling in front of them, patting his son's knee. In a stern voice Charles said, "Tell me what happened. Did that man hurt you?"

Charles tried again to get his son to talk. "Why did you go outside?"

Jack stared at his father, then at his mother. Mary rubbed the boy's arm.

"It's ok, son. Papa isn't angry at you."

Jack sniffed, looked at his father and frowned. "Don't know."

"Did that man hurt you?" asked Charles again.

Jack shook his head. "I was scared."

"That doesn't surprise me," Mary said. "Robert is not a nice man and he is very large."

Emma could stand it no longer. "I think there is some misunderstanding. Robert only wanted to help. Why do you distrust him so?"

"You don't know what Robert was thinking, Emma. Men have been known to kidnap children. His prior strange actions speak louder than his words. I think there is something wrong with the man." Charles turned back to his son. "In the future, young man, you are not to go out at night. Nor should you ever go near Robert's property. When you do go outside in the daylight, be sure you let one of us go with you."

Jack nodded his head.

"Well, let's eat before the dinner gets cold."

Emma sat down in her chair, her mind repeating what had just happened. She saw it differently than her hosts. She would somehow get to the bottom of this mystery.

SEVEN

RABBITS

The next morning after Charles had gone to work and Mary was busy with the baby, Emma sat in the back parlor watching Jack. He was still upset about what happened the night before and wanted someone with him. He had followed Mary around most of the morning like a pet dog. Mary finally asked Emma to take Jack into the back parlor and distract him for a while. Emma had picked up the boy and hugged him while he cried in her arms, not wanting to be separated from his mother. She then sat him on the floor and sat next to him in a parlor chair and encouraged him to play with his blocks. Jack finally calmed down and later rode his rocking horse. It was his favorite toy. Emma believed someday he would rock back and forth so hard the horse would tip over. She watched the boy for a moment. She then got up and walked towards Jack and stood next to him.

She whispered quietly to him, "Jack, why did you leave the house last night?"

The boy stopped his rocking and looked at Emma. She smiled at him and tried to encourage him to speak.

"I saw Socks."

Jack had been scolded many times by his father to leave the wild rabbits in the yard alone and not to chase them. But Jack could not help himself. He wanted one for a pet and often when outside and chased them. Emma had seen him do it on many occasions. The animals, however, always got away, they being quicker than the small boy. Emma and Jack had named one brown rabbit with white feet 'Socks.' Emma had been teaching Jack just to watch the rabbit by making up stories about the bunny and how Socks didn't like to be chased.

"And you chased him."

Jack lowered his head.

Emma placed her hand under the child's chin and lifted his head up. She asked again. " Did you chase the rabbit?"

Jack looked her in the eye and nodded.

"Where did he go?"

Jack pushed her hand from his face. "The barn."

"You mean your father's stable, the one at the end of the property? That is a long way for a rabbit to run." Charles kept his two horses in the stable. The building was a good fifty feet from the house.

Jack shook his head. "The other one." His mouth trembled a bit in response.

The other barn must be Robert's. It was a small shed that was in the center of the man's garden. It was a poor dwelling compared to Charles' fine stable. Emma thought about yesterday's event. Robert's house had no lights on and the garden would have been very dark once Jack had run over there away from the Cooper's house. There had been clouds in the sky last night, and Emma remembered how even Robert's form had been barely visible in the dark. It had been very difficult to see anything.

Emma rubbed the little boy's back with her hand. "You must have been very afraid in the dark."

Jack's head shot up and he looked into Emma's eyes. A look of understanding went between them.

"I was."

Emma continued to rub the boy's back. "Did you cry?"

Jack nodded again. "Then the bad man found me."

Emma had to bite her tongue to keep from correcting the little boy, but it would do her no good to go against her cousin's reasoning.

"It's best you don't chase rabbits anymore," she said instead.

Jack stopped his rocking on his horse and smiled shyly at Emma in response.

"Would you like to help me make dinner?"

Jack got off his horse and followed Emma into the kitchen. Emma had decided to make a chicken pie for supper. She had prepared the chicken ahead of time by boiling a young bird in a pot with just enough water to cover it. When the meat was tender, she had removed the chicken from the stove. She picked the meat from the bones and put it on a plate. Now she and Jack would make a pie crust.

Emma didn't need a cook book to instruct her on how to form the crust. She had made many fruit and meat pies at home and knew the recipe by heart.

She lifted the boy and stood him on a chair near the table where she planned to work on the meal. She brought a bowl over and placed a quarter pound of lard and the same amount of butter in it. She then helped Jack pour a pound of flour into the mixture. His little hands were soon white as snow.

Emma's hands covered Jack's small ones on the large wooden spoon that they held. Together they stirred the shortening and the flour until it was well mixed. Jack thought this was a fine game and giggled in pleasure. Emma added a little salt and just enough water to make the flour turn into dough that was able to be rolled out flat.

She placed part of the rolled-out dough in a large pudding pan. Then Jack and she put the chicken pieces over the crust with a few slices of pork. She added a little chicken broth and a dash of butter before covering it with the top layer of crust. She placed their pie in the stove, then cleaned up Jack.

At dinner Charles exclaimed that the meat pie was the best he had ever eaten. Jack beamed at his father and said he helped make it.

EIGHT

IN THE GARDEN

Emma awoke to a cry. At first she was not sure what it was. It came again. The scream was loud and pierced the quiet of her bedroom.

She opened her eyes and rolled over in her bed, thinking it was the cry of the newborn baby. She wondered why Mary didn't tend to the little girl. The cry came again, shrill as if someone was in agony. Emma sat upright in her bed, shaking at the sound. The cry stopped. Its sound came not from within the quiet house, but from the night outside. She rose from her bed, the chill of the darkness grabbing hold of her the moment she shed her comforter and blankets.

She looked outside. The full moon lit the yard of the house next door. She saw a movement near the trees, a figure walking about in the distance. She heard him cry again. Was it Jack? Had he let the house again?

Quickly she put on her coat and shoes. She crept down the stairs, being careful not to wake the others. Her shoes made soft thumping noises on the wood staircase and floor.

She stepped out the back door of her cousin's house. The blackness of the night surrounded her. She could barely make out the shadows of the trees.

"Jack," she called, "where are you?" Why had the boy left the house again? Surely he was not outside chasing rabbits. She stumbled in the dark, almost falling, until she saw a human figure hunched over like a small round ball. Her concern for him blocked out any fright or thought of danger she might have.

"Jack are you hurt?" The quietness of the night echoed her words.

The form rose to his full height. It towered over Emma, black and menacing.

"Who's there?" an angry voice answered in reply.

It wasn't Jack at all, but Robert. She recognized his voice. The tone of his voice sent a chill down her back. Was he drunk or deranged? She stopped frozen in her tracks, like an animal of prey caught in the presence of its attacker. She knew not what to do, to flee or stay.

He moved in front of her, separating her from her cousin's house, her place of safety. She felt trapped. She remembered her father's voice saying," When in the present of a wild animal, don't run. Don't show them that you are afraid."

"Who's there?" he repeated. "Don't come any closer or I will use my gun."

Emma eyes grew wide with fear. Her mouth went dry, as she tried to find the voice that seemed to have jammed in her throat.

"It's me. Emma," she whispered.

"Who?"

"Emma," she said louder this time. "Emma, from the stagecoach."

Emma stood stone still. She waited. The minutes seemed like hours as she waited for his reply. She was suddenly aware of wearing only her nightgown under her coat and how indecent that was. Tension filled the air. She felt it all round her. She dared not move. What would her cousin think if she found her shot in the middle of Robert's garden? Perhaps their opinion of Robert was correct.

She could see the outline of his stocky figure through the moonlight moving closer. He held a revolver in his hand. It was pointed at her. She stared at the gun, fear pulsing through her veins like blood. She stepped slowly backward, hoping not to entice his anger. But still he came towards her. She stepped back again and found that she had backed herself right against a big tree trunk. Terrified, she swallowed hard and prepared to die. She closed her eyes and asked her Maker to receive her soul.

"Emma." His voice had softened and no longer sounded alarmed. He peered at her through the darkness to see if it was really her. "What are you doing out in the night?"

Emma took a deep breath, opened her eyes and realized the danger had past. Her body relaxed. Until this moment she hadn't realized she had been holding her breath.

"Emma?" He repeated her name as if he had just heard it for the first time. "Answer me."

"I heard your cry and thought it was Jack."

Robert moved one more step forward, until he was inches from her. She felt his hot breath upon her face and smelled his presence. What would he do now?

"Yes, it is me. Emma," she said.

He seemed to go limp when he recognized her. His shoulder, once tight and alert dropped several inches. The gun he held in his hand that had been pointed at her, he slowly lowered to his side. Tears of relief dripped down her face as she stared at the gun, her body shaking.

"Emma." He shook his head. "You shouldn't be out here. It's not safe."

She thought about his words as she stood there, wondering exactly what he meant. Was there someone else lurking around in the dark? She saw no other shadows and heard only the rattling of the wind through the trees.

"Why are you in the garden? Who do you fear?"

He sighed, his mouth tightening until it was a straight line. "Myself," he said at last. "The memories of dead soldiers haunt my dreams at night and have given me no peace. My mind is full of them. I can't make them go away. I came outside in hope that the cold air would clear my head, or that I might end this torture in another way."

Emma looked again at the firearm he held in his hand. She gasped as she came to fully understand his words and fear came back again. She put a hand on his arm.

"You must not think that way."

But he jerked his arm away. "You wouldn't understand about death, and I need not burden you with my troubles. Go back into the house. Leave me now to deal with these ghosts."

Emma didn't take a step. She could hear something in his voice, something desperate and unnerving. She listened to his ragged breathing, as if he had run a long way. She knew something was very wrong. Maybe, it was because she could not see his face clearly in the dark that she was aware of his very essence, his wounded mind and heart.

"I know about death," she said. "And how it leaves invisible scars on the living. My brother Alfred fought for the Union in the war. He was captured and held at Anderson prison in the South. He died from complications due to his wounds. And my sister just two months ago died from La Grippe. I understand more than you know. I know that empty feeling that burns in my heart that never goes away. I know how days can feel bleak and without purpose."

Robert stepped back and stared at her, his eyes wide with surprise. He stepped away from her. He found a stump of a tree and sat down. His voice changed once more to eerie calm.

"I am sorry that one as young as you has gone through such pain. Perhaps you have known death more intimately than I thought and know how it changes you. I was not much older than you are now when I joined the Union army to fight in the great war. It seemed like a wise choice back then. I needed the money. I had not been in the army very long. In fact, I hadn't even fired the gun they issued me when the war found me.

We were camped at Pittsburg Landing, Tennessee, near a church called Shiloh. There were hundreds, no, thousands of us Union soldiers there. Soldiers as far as the eye could see. We had been camping out in the open. I was finishing breakfast, enjoying the orchards. The dogwoods were in bloom and the forest floor carpeted in violets. Birds were singing.

"Suddenly the Confederate soldiers attacked us with an army as big or bigger than ours. They emerged from the woods in a long line, banners waving and guns firing. My commander ordered us forward. The man next to me took a bullet to his chest and he fell to the ground. We were unprepared for the attack and retreated back towards the river. I can hear the sounds of the weapons and men screaming still today. We found cover in an old sunken road and fired back at them. We fought long into the night and the next day. A body of a dead soldier lay next to me for most of the fight, his arm ripped off by a cannonball. I remember the ugly smell of combat, smoke and blood.

"Our reinforcements came the next day and the confederate soldiers, outnumbered, departed. Some of my Iowa friends died that day. Why I did not, I know not. I was not even wounded."

He shook his head in disbelief. He took a breath and then continued.

"The next morning bodies without arms and legs, some burned along with dead horses, lay across the battlefield. Some lay in heaps. The battlefield was five miles square and everywhere you stepped there were the dead. This sight was almost more horrible than the battle itself. I watched as men buried the dead in large dug-out trenches in the ground. They would put fifty to a hundred bodies in a pit as if they were spoiled meat. I hope never to see such things again. Yet I do. I live with the war inside me. I hear the sounds. I smell the odors. It never leaves me alone for long. Like tonight, the ghosts come back to haunt me. There are days when I envy the dead. At least their pain is gone, but mine continues."

Emma didn't move. She let his words flow through her. The horror of his words reached her heart and she wondered why he had unburdened himself to her this night. Her body trembled, not because of the cold of night but by his words. How could anyone bear such suffering? She felt compassion for the man next to her, but she was wise enough to know that words would not take away his pain.

She whispered to him, "I often wonder why my sister died at such a young age and not me. It seems unfair. She was young and full of life. Yet I go on living in hope that I shall one day find the purpose that God has for me. I haven't found it yet. But I feel he has left me on this earth for some reason. This hope keeps me going when I find myself in those moments of despair and the pain tries to overcome me. I find it takes courage to go on living."

Robert rose from the stump and came to her.

"Tonight you are an angel that has rescued me from myself. It is time for you to return to the house before you fall ill to the cold."

He took her arm and gently walked her to her cousin's house. Emma tugged her coat around her and let him guide her back through the gardens. They walked in silence. At the entranceway to the house, she stopped.

"How will I know that you made it through this night? For I will not sleep soundly again worrying about you and your ghosts."

The moonlight shone brightly on his face and she could see his brown eyes. He looked deeply into hers.

"I would not want you to be disturbed. Tomorrow when you wake, look out the window when the sun rises and I will wave to you as I go on my way to work. I will wave every day hereafter so your mind need not be troubled. Which window is your room?"

Emma pointed to the window on the top floor.

"What is it that you do for a living?"

"I am a carpenter."

Emma nodded. She then walked through the door of her cousin's house. Quietly she made her way to her bedroom. She was surprised that no one else had woken up. She tossed her coat and shoes aside and crawled back into bed. She drew the comforter over her body. She did not sleep for a long time. Her mind was full of thoughts.

NINE

THE WINDOW

Robert went back into his house. He had entered by the back door. The room that had seemed too small and confining just moments ago now seemed welcoming. The room breathed of safety. He walked the familiar path to his bed. Even in the dark he knew the way. He threw his body onto the mattress and stared into the darkness, fearing that the battlefield of war would find him. But the room stayed as it was, and he heard only the creaking of the boards as the wind blew. He closed his eyes and still his mind stayed steady. Find God's purpose?

I was left on this earth for some reason.

Her words echoed in his ears. He had never met this God that Emma talked about, and he was not sure he could believe that every event in life had a reason. In fact, the battle that haunted him had started on a Sunday, the Lord's Day, not far from a Methodist chapel. Perhaps Emma would change her mind about her God, if she knew this fact.

He turned over in his bed and lay on his side. He was more inclined to believe in the devil than in a loving God, for he had seen firsthand the evil that men did on this earth. He could not wrap his mind around the idea that human beings could be so unkind and believed instead some evil spirit filled them to commit such evil acts. A good spirit would not permit the horrors he had seen. Purpose? Even in his deranged state, was there still a purpose he was yet to fulfil? These thoughts lured him into sleep, and he dreamed no more that night.

The next morning Robert pulled on his clothes, ate a piece of bread for breakfast, and hurried out the door. He thought about the night that had passed and his conversation with Emma. Never had he told a soul about what he had seen during the war. He feared what people would think of him. Never had he wanted another person to hear such tales, fearing they would not understand. Yet Emma, little Emma, had not shied away from truth. Nor had she cringed from the horror. Her own story of loss had given him courage to share his own pain. He couldn't believe the mercy and compassion he had felt coming from her. Her concern for him had radiated from her. She was a rare woman, and he vowed to get to know her better.

True to his promise, when he stepped outside his house the next morning, he looked up at the second floor window in the Cooper's house. He was stunned to see Emma sitting there, her face pressed to the glass. He had not really thought she would do as he had said. But there she was, waiting for a sign from him that he was fine. He wondered how long she had been sitting there waiting for him to appear. It warmed his heart to think that someone cared enough to worry about him. He had been alone for many years, and other than when he was in the war, he had no one to check on his coming and his going. He lifted his hand and waved. Emma waved back and for a moment the day seemed brighter, the world a less hostile place.

Emma had slept restlessly through the night. She worried about Robert and what he might do. In her mind, she saw the gun in his hand and she saw the blank, sad look in his eyes. She tossed and turned in her blankets until they were twisted around her body. Her thoughts gave her no peace.

When she could stand it no longer, she got up out of bed. She pulled a chair over to the window and wrapped the bed comforter around her. She stared out into the black of night and waited for the light of day. She must have dozed off, for she awoke with a jerk when the sun shone in her eyes. She opened them just in time to see Robert wave at her. She waved back. A great feeling of relief flooded through her body.

For the next two weeks, every morning she rose and went to the window and looked out. Sometimes she had to wait a long time for Robert to appear. At such times her heart would beat rapidly within her chest, wondering what had become of him. But he always showed up. Never did he miss a day.

As time went on she grew to worry less and came to enjoy their morning ritual. It gave her something to look forward to each day. The more she thought about Robert, the fonder she became of him. Only a kind man who thought about others more than himself would seek to ease her mind with such a friendly gesture each day. She sensed that he, too, started to enjoy himself. One morning he tipped his hat to her instead of waving. Another day he bowed to her. Another morning she found him sitting on the porch steps and he pointed to his pocket watch when she appeared, as if to say where have you been and why are you late? She shrugged her shoulders in response.

She started to return his playfulness. Some days she would fix her hair into one braid and pin it on top of her head and put on her best dress. Other days she brushed her hair in front of her shoulders and let it hang down passed her breasts. One morning she saluted him after he saluted her.

During the day as she did her chores and played with Jack, she found herself humming. She daydreamed about what Robert was doing. Was he pounding nails into a fine piece of wood or putting in a window in a house? She knew little about what carpenters did but marveled at the buildings they put up.

Time passed quickly, and she never again heard Robert prowling in his garden at night. She took this as a good sign, even though he seemed to still work late at night. Many times when she looked out her window before she went bed, she found his house dark. Where was he? Or did he just use a single candle to light his way in his home? She found this thought disturbing.

TEN

TRIP TO TOWN

"Emma," Mary said, thrusting a few coins into her hand. "Be sure to go talk to Martha, my dressmaker, and pick out material for a new dress. It is my payment to you for all the hard work you have done around the house."

"It was no trouble," Emma said. "I have enjoyed my time here." She tried to push the money back into her cousin's hand. But Mary refused to take it.

"Charles and I talked it over. We insist you do as we say."

Charles appeared in the doorway of the house. He held in his hand the supply list his wife had provided for him.

"The carriage is ready. Are you?" He directed the question to Emma.

"I am," Emma said and followed him out the door. Charles was taking her into town. Emma could barely contain the excitement that bubbled inside of her as she rode in the buggy beside him. She had not been to town since the day she had arrived and was looking forward to exploring the city.

They quickly left the housing area. Charles drove the horse

and carriage on Water Street along the Des Moines River, one of the two rivers that bisected the town. Green grass could be seen starting to grow on its banks, and Emma saw the bridge she had crossed upon her arrival. A few boats floated on the river, a brisk breeze rippling the water beneath them. They turned onto Court Avenue past the brick structures and arrived at Second Street.

Charles stopped the buggy and helped her to the ground. Emma had been told by Mary that many of the best stores were between Court Avenue and Market Street. The Des Moines business area was compact and located in the center of town, while the family homes were scattered far back from the main streets of town in the gently rolling hills. The houses were often hidden from view by the trees. Farms and prairies were further out. The town itself was two and half miles from north to south and four and a half miles east to west.

She looked down Court Avenue. Two-story and three-story brick buildings lined the street on each side, with occasional single-story dwellings between them. At the end of the street, five blocks from where she stood, was the public square and the courthouse. Charles had told her many tales about the courthouse during her stay and she was glad to finally see it for herself. It was a two-story building which featured a dome on its top and four roman pillars near its doors. Two alabaster statues of Liberty and Justice flanked the doors as well. The courthouse yard was surrounded by an ornamental iron fence, and within its bounds was a fountain where four iron geese floated in the basin, spraying water from their long necks.

Construction on the building had started in 1858, but due to the Civil War it was not occupied until 1868. Cost for the building had reached ninety-four thousand dollars. Charles said it was poorly made and even though it had been open just a year, it required repairs. The courtroom inside was sixty feet square and could seat a thousand people, which made the courthouse the largest public hall in Des Moines. The jail was in the basement of the courthouse, and its prisoners sent up unpleasant smells to the floors above, as well as some drunken songs.

Charles called the courthouse an architectural monstrosity. From where Emma stood, it looked quite impressive.

Charles pointed down Second Street. "Martha's dress shop is not far from Woodward & Hepburn fancy dry goods store and John McWilliams groceries." Emma looked in the direction he pointed. "It has a sign on the door that says 'Taylors' and is located in a small, one-story wood building. It's easy to find. When you're finished shopping, you can meet me at my office on Fourth Street."

Emma nodded her head as his carriage soon mingled with the other wagons on Court Avenue. She also noticed the street railroad coach that was pulled by a team of horses. Shoppers in Des Moines could catch a ride in a coach that ran on rails down Court Avenue west from Capitol Hill to 5th Street. The coach ran daily.

She listened to the noises of the city. A horse neighed and wagons groaned as they made their way to their destinations. She walked along the dusty road, watching where she stepped to avoid droppings from the horses. She passed Child, Sanford Hardware shop and couldn't resist and went inside. This large store had a little of everything; hoes, shovels and spades hung on the wall. Two stoves and some agricultural implements sat on the floor. She spied a section of the shop full of cooking equipment and house furnishings. She wandered around the items and wished she could buy some new pans for her mother. Her mother's cooking equipment was old and worn. Far in the back of the store she smelled leather and saw a saddle, harness and carriage trimmings. Not far from them were latches, screws, saws, and anvils. The farm equipment made her think of her father, who would be waiting for good weather to put in his crops. She walked out of the store.

She had never been to a dressmaker. Her mother had made all of her clothes. She had tried to convince her cousin, Mary, to just allow her to pick out some fabric at a home furnishing store and take it back to her mother. But Mary had insisted she go to Martha.

"You will like her," Mary explained. "The dressmaker knows all the latest fashions and makes the most beautiful garments. All the town people go to her."

Emma found the tiny shop nestled between two larger brick buildings. She went inside. She looked around. Two forms with dresses on them stood just inside the door. Bolts of colorful cloth lay on shelves just behind them. A few pieces of lace had fallen on the floor, along with strands of threads and small scraps of cloth. The walls of the shop were painted white. The small room was clean and tidy.

A slim woman about fifty years old, with glasses on her face and dressed in a dark blue gown, sat behind a machine where she had been working. Black material flowed off one side of the machine. The woman's foot pushed a pedal beneath the machine. Emma walked closer and she saw a metal base and arm on the machine. A needle from the arm moved up and down with the rhythm of Martha's foot. The woman stopped her labor and looked up.

"Can I help you?" she said with a thick English accent.

Emma smiled at the woman. Her mother had that same strong accent.

"I'm Emma. Mary Cooper is my cousin. She sent me."

The woman stood and Emma discovered that the woman was not much taller than herself, but much thinner. Her mother would have said a good wind could have blown the woman away.

"Nice to meet you." Martha said. "Mary is a nice lady. I've made several dresses for her. What kind of dress are you wanting?" The woman walked towards her. Emma could see a few deep wrinkles lining her face and raised veins on the back of her hands. The woman had known hard work, Emma reasoned.

"A good dress. Something for special occasions."

Martha smiled. A bright spark twinkled in her eye. She motioned to the dresses on the cloth dummies.

"Something like this?"

Emma walked closer to the dresses on the forms. One was a gray, three-piece silk dress with a design of brown and white flowers woven in the material. It had long sleeves, a high collar, and the straight bodice narrowed at the waist. An over-shirt overlapped the lined shirt. The front of the bodice fastened with hooks and six gray silk decorative buttons. The skirt was full with volumes of material. A small bustle that sat high at the back of the dress caused the skirt to hang further from the body. Its length was long, and the back material of the dress formed a train that would drag on the ground. The bodice and overskirt were trimmed with a deep brown silk ribbon.

Emma could see her cousin Mary wearing such a dress, but it had too many pieces for her. She turned to the other one. It, too, had a bodice trimmed with lace. Its underskirt fell in multiple layers of ruffles and flounces. The overskirt was pulled up in the back to reveal the fancy underskirt, and the skirt's material again produced a small train. The dress was a deep blue velvet.

Emma frowned. "These are beautiful." Emma had never seen anything so grand. She spoke slowly, not wanting to disappoint the woman. "I'm a country girl. I need something simple."

She could not imagine wearing such dresses visiting a neighbor or attending a Sunday service. Country folks did not get away from their homes much. A special occasion dress was just one that was not worn every day and kept clean for occasional use.

"Ah, a practical girl you are. Let me take your measurements and I will think upon it awhile." The woman stood next to Emma and taking a string, she wrapped it around Emma's breast, then her waist and hips.

"You have a small waist. The latest fashion likes a tight, narrow-waist bodice. Perhaps we could do a one-piece dress. A bodice with an overskirt attached and a straight, not too full underskirt whose hem is a few inches from the ground, about the length your skirt is now. There will be one ruffle at the bottom. I will put lace at the high collar near the throat and around the sleeves for decoration. The color is what will make this dress. I think a beautiful emerald green will set off your hair. The material will be of moderate weight so you can wear it anytime, summer or winter."

Emma looked a little doubtful. Most dresses were made of dark colors.

Martha walked to a table and looked through papers there, then brought out one to show Emma. It was a drawing from a dress pattern made by Ellen Curtis Demorest. Emma liked the look of the dress, but was still hesitant about the color.

"Don't worry," Martha said. "You will like it. Trust me. Come back in a week for a fitting?"

"You can make a dress in a week?" Emma thought about her mother slaving for hours and days with a thread and needle.

Martha nodded. "I have a sewing machine. It cuts down on the time considerably."

Emma's head was spinning with all the new information she had discovered today, sewing machines, dress patterns.

"I bought mine from the Bartholomew & Cole Company. Their shop is on 6th Street if you are interested in one. They cost a lot, but I had to have one after I saw it demonstrated at the State Fair last year."

So that was what Martha had been doing when Emma entered the shop, sewing on the sewing machine. She had heard about such things as sewing machines but had never seen one until today. They were a new machine she had read about in the newspaper. She eyed the machine in wonderment. Ah, if she could only sew and make beautiful things like Martha and her mother, what a grand purpose in life that would be. But Emma could barely thread a needle or mend a garment, much less make a dress. She had once sewn a sleeve in wrong. Her mother had to tear it all out and redo it.

"You're all thumbs," her mother had remarked to her.

Martha dismissed Emma with a wave of her hand. Emma left the shop. She walked back to Court Avenue and strolled south.

She entered several shops and bought a bag of candy for Jack. She had little money and was saving most of it for her dress. Each purchase she made she thought long and hard about. Even though she bought little, she enjoyed looking and dreaming of owning such wonderful things.

Besides retail stores, there were several saloons along the way. They caused nothing but trouble. Men getting drunk at night. Mary and several women groups were encouraging the local politicians to consider prohibitions to cut down on such activities. Mary had told Emma there were forty-one liquor dealers in town, way too many for a town the size of Des Moines.

A hand touched her shoulder and she jumped back away from the touch.

"Looking for a bonnet, Miss?" came a male voice.

Emma turned around to face the voice. "Robert!" she exclaimed. "You scared me."

Emma looked into his glowing brown eyes. She noticed an amused grin on his lips. She could not help but grin back at him. She was glad to see him.

"No, I have not bought a bonnet, but I have ordered a dress."

"I would like very much to see you in it," Robert said.

"Perhaps you shall," Emma replied. His comment had pleased her. For a moment she imagined dancing with Robert in her stunning new dress.

"I saw you from across the street and ran to catch up with you. Perhaps we could walk a while together."

"I would like that," she replied. Emma had many questions to ask him. Why was he in town? How did he find her? She kept them to herself. She became aware of his broad chest and tall male figure towering beside her. She felt her physical attraction to him and she suddenly became unnaturally shy. She was not sure what to do with the feeling.

He fell into step beside her and shortened his strides to match her own. He looked down at her with a radiant smile on his face. They said not a word for several blocks, but it didn't seem to matter. They were content, in a fog of happiness all their own.

"Have you seen any ghosts lately?" she asked.

"They seemed to have left me for a while," he responded. "I never know exactly when they will reappear. A certain smell, a boom of thunder, or noise from a gun seems to summon them. Mostly they come at night in my dreams, and I relive the horror of the war."

She still marveled that he had told her his dark thoughts that fated night. But because he had, they had a bond. The bond joined them together, each willing to help the other.

"Then we will have to enjoy the sun."

"Yes, we must."

They walked a while further. He pointed out to her the first buildings of Des Moines and some of the dwellings he had a hand in constructing. The town had doubled its population these last three years. He told her about the town's history. The town had started out as a fort along the Des Moines River. In 1853 by an act of the legislature, Fort Des Moines had been incorporated into a city.

She in turn chattered about the things that had happened to her in the Cooper's household, the funny things that Jack said, and of the cake she made that refused to rise. He laughed and told her he would have eaten it anyway.

He suddenly grabbed her arm to halt her progress. She stumbled into him. Her body brushed his. He bent down and picked up a coin partly hidden in the dirt. He rubbed it on his pant leg to clean the dust from it.

"A bit of silver for you."

He placed it in her hand. She wrapped her fingers around it. She then raised it to her face and studied it. An eagle was printed on one side of the coin with the words, United States of America, and beneath the eagle the words *One Dol.* The words circled around the coin's edges. In small letters on a banner near the eagle's head were the words "In God We Trust". She turned the coin over and found a woman sitting down, and beneath her the numbers 1870.

Emma looked at the fountain with statues of geese spouting water. They had reached the front of the courthouse. A building built for truth and justice. She had had little money in her life and this silver dollar was like a gift from heaven. Whoever lost it would be sad indeed.

She shook her head. "It is very kind of you to give it to me. Are you sure you don't want to keep it?" But she hoped he would say no. She wanted it as keepsake, as a remembrance of this day.

"It is yours," he said. "Do with it as you please. Which way now?"

"To Charles' office. It's on Walnut Street and Fourth Street."

He tucked his hand under her arm and they turned right and walked one block. They then headed north. As they walked they passed Stamper Brothers Photography shop. Robert encouraged her to get her photograph taken one day. He had one taken when he was in the war and sent it back home to his parents.

"My brother Alfred had done the same," Emma remarked. She was glad that he had, for when he died, they had something to remember him by.

The Union Restaurant and Saloon was doing a lively business as they strolled by. Further down the street, Emma saw the newspaper shops. She counted five. Des Moines townsfolk must be well–read, she figured.

They soon arrived at a stately two-story brick building not far from where the Savery Hotel was being constructed. She was glad Robert was with her. She would not have found this address on her own.

"Go through the door up the stairs. First office on the left belongs to Charles."

She stood in front of Robert looking up at him. She didn't want this day to end. She was happy, a feeling she had not felt since her sister had died. The whole day had been pleasant.

"Will you come up with me?"

Robert stood awkwardly wringing his hands as if he knew not what to do.

"I fear I would not be welcome."

Emma nodded. Then leaning forward, she stood on her tiptoes and gently kissed his cheek. She then quickly turned away before he could say a word.

Emma sighed and opened the tall oak door. She mounted the stairs inside the entranceway and marched up them in a rush. She was tempted to linger a while longer with Robert, but she knew Charles was expecting her.

Emma entered his office and found him standing near the window not far from his desk. In his gray suit he presented an imposing figure. In his hand he held a walking cane and tapped it lightly in his other hand. He turned, his eyes blazing with fury and his face taut with anger.

"You do not know what you are doing Emma! I saw you with him. I fear you are getting tangled up in a situation you will regret."

Charles' loud voice made her stop. The blood in her face drained away, turning it white. He had seen her. The kiss had been a private gesture not meant for others' eyes.

"How dare you display such affection in pubic. It is inappropriate. What else have you been doing while under my roof?"

Anger started to boil inside Emma. She could not hold her

tongue. Charles was an opinionated fool. She crossed her arms and held her ground. She straightened herself to her full height. She tried to make herself as tall as possible.

"You know him not, Charles." Her voice was low. "He is a war hero. You have no right to condemn the man without even speaking to him."

"Is that what he told you, that he is a hero? How naïve can you be?"

"Any man who returns from war and has faced the blazing of guns is a hero in my book." Her voice had raised in volume.

Charles continue to tap his cane, this time on the floor, his mouth opened slightly at her words.

"And you have spoken to him about the war? No man should share such things with a woman."

"I have," she replied. "I find him a worthy man."

Charles walked towards her. "While you are in my house, I forbid you to speak to him again."

Emma saw the anger in his eyes. For a moment she felt threatened and alarmed. Charles' large form loomed over her, his cane clutched tightly in his hand. For a moment she thought he might strike her with it. She watched him closely to see what movement he would make. She hoped to ease the tension in the room and meekly said, "I will do as you wish. I meant no harm."

He turned to look out the window and muttered, "It is good that you will be leaving soon. Your mother wrote us recently. She misses you and wants you to return. We will no longer be needing your help in a week or two. Mary has recovered nicely."

He stood still for several minutes as if deep in thought. He turned to face her once again, then rustled some papers on the desk. He picked up one and handed it to her.

"I don't know if this is wise after what I just saw outside. However, I did speak to Mr. Allen, a wealthy man of influence in town, about you. He will be looking for a second cook for his new house this fall. I mentioned you were handy in the kitchen and might be interested in the positon. Here's his address if you care to call on him. However, now I don't know if it is such a good idea. You may be better off in your parents' home."

Tears stung Emma eyes. His words struck as if she had been hit in the stomach, knocking the air from her lungs. She hated Charles at that moment and wanted to hurt him as he had hurt her. But she held her tongue. A cook. She had hoped for something better, a teacher perhaps. He thought of her as a servant and someone to order around.

But she took the paper and tried to make the best of it. She wondered how her cousin could put up with such an arrogant man. The thought of her leaving was almost more than she could imagine at this moment. When would she ever see Robert again? Perhaps this position as a cook would give her a reason to return.

Her mouth trembled. She quietly said, "Thank you. I will sit in your front room until you are ready to go home."

She turned her back on him and could still feel his eyes glaring at her. She walked woodenly to a chair and sat stiff and proud. She waited an hour. By that time her anger had been spent and she wondered how to make amends. She would talk to Mary.

ELEVEN

THE LETTER

Mary was appalled at Emma's actions and took the side of her husband, Charles. She lectured Emma on the ways of men and how stupid Emma had been to kiss Robert. Emma could take it no more and revealed to Mary the night she discovered Robert in the garden. Instead of calming her cousin's fears, the story alarmed Mary even more.

"You could have been shot!" She scolded Emma once again for her foolish behavior. Emma could only say she had not done it on purpose. She had thought Jack was in trouble.

For the rest of Emma's stay, Mary did not let her out of her sight. Mary sat in the kitchen when Emma cooked. She was there when Emma played with Jack. Mary even escorted Emma to her room when she retired for the night. But Emma hadn't told her about waving at Robert in the morning. Emma cherished those simple moments even more now and vowed never to tell Mary her secret.

When Emma had to return to the dressmaker for her final fitting a week later, Mary accompanied her. Mary left the children in care of the mid-wife, Mrs. Bishop. Emma thought that Mary enjoyed the outing more than she did. Mary chatted happily to her husband as they rode to town. Emma sat quietly in the back of the carriage and tried to capture in her memory the town of Des Moines. Charles waited with the horse and carriage as Mary and Emma entered the dressmaker's shop.

Martha greeted them with a joyful hello, then set about getting Emma's dress and helping her put it on. The dress fit perfectly.

"Oh my, all the women in Mount Pleasant will be envious of you," Mary remarked as Emma viewed herself in a mirror and slowly turned in a circle. Emma had to agree the dress made her look quite pretty. The color set off her hair and eyes. The foot-tall ruffle at the bottom of the dress and the white lace on the cuffs and neck made the dress look elegant. Martha got on her knees in front of Emma and pinned in the hem. When Martha had finished, Emma walked to her cousin and gave her a hug.

"I'm grateful for the dress, Cousin," she said and meant the words with her whole heart. Never had she had such a fine dress.

Mary eyes sparkled with pleasure. "You're welcome, Emma. You earned it."

Emma paid Martha for the dress and then changed back into her other clothes.

"I can sew in the hem today, and the dress should be done by the time you finish your shopping." Martha placed the dress on her sewing machine. Emma looked at Mary to see if this was a good decision.

"We will be back in an hour or two," Mary replied.

Against Emma's wishes, Mary and Charles insisted that they stop at Mr. B. Franklin Allen's house on Fourth Street, just off

Court Avenue not far from the court house. They wanted Emma to speak to him about the cook positon and learn more about what her duties might be. Emma forced a smile onto her lips in response and tried to be agreeable. She sat in the back of the carriage and said not a word as Mary and Charles lectured her on the merits of the job and the history of the couple she was to meet.

Benjamin Franklin Allen was the nephew of Captain James Allen, who had chosen the site for the fort that had been become the town of Des Moines. Troops were stationed there to keep settlers off the land until October 1845, when a large tract of land passed from the Sauk and Meskwaki Indians to the United States. Benjamin Franklin Allen, at the age of nineteen, inherited some funds from his uncle when he died in 1846. He showed great ambition, even at that age, and started a general store in Des Moines with a partner and later started a bank. He became a director of an insurance company, the railroad, and the gas company. He had even served a term in the Iowa Senate. He was well thought of by most people in Des Moines and helped many get loans for their houses and businesses. He was also involved in charities such as the Civil War orphan homes.

"You have no idea what a good opportunity this is for you, Emma," Mary explained. "The Allens are one of the finest families in town. His wife, Arathusa, is a wonderful woman. I met her at one of the receptions held at their house a couple of years ago. If you get this position, you will also be living with them."

"The Allens," Charles said, "have built a new house west of town. "It is considerably bigger than this one, and that is why they will need more staff."

"The newspapers have printed stories about the new house. I can't wait to see it when it is finished," added Mary.

Emma nodded in response and tried to show some excitement. But she remembered a story her older brother had told when she was young. Her family had traveled from England to the United States when she was a child. Her brother, ten years older than she, had come to the States a year prior to their arrival.

Before coming to America, he had worked as a footman in a huge country manor while in England and had desired something better for himself than a domestic servant. He had wanted to buy land of his own, and Iowa's territory had just opened up. He had jumped at the opportunity to come here.

He had told Emma stories about his time as a footman. He had warned her that one of the hardest jobs in the manor was the cook. The cook spent long hours in the kitchen making three meals a day for the owner's family as well as the other servants. The cook was on her feet all day, barely taking a break to rest. When company came to visit, she was under great stress to prepare fancy meals.

"If you must become a domestic servant be anything but the cook," he warned. His words echoed in Emma's ears as she listened to her cousin's chatter.

They all got out of the carriage and Charles knocked on the door of a fine, two-story brick house. Emma followed behind her cousin and her husband. Emma had hoped to find a job teaching children in a school instead of a cook position. Unknown to her relatives, she had copied down the names and addresses of the directors of schools in Des Moines from a City Directory book Charles had left on the table in the front parlor. She planned to write them all a letter as soon as she returned home. Because

Charles had been excited about the cook's position, she had not told him or Mary her plan.

A maid came to the door and told them that the Allens were not at home and they had gone on a trip to Chicago to buy furniture for their new home. Charles and Mary let out a sigh of disappointment, but Emma took it as an omen. The position was not meant for her. The only good thing about the position, Emma thought, was that it might have given her an opportunity to see Robert again. That would have made it all worthwhile. She hid her smile as they walked back to their carriage.

Emma could not take the joyful conversation between Mary and Charles on the way home. She wished someday she could share with a man the same harmony the couple seemed to exhibit. Her single status seemed dismal indeed today, and she had doubts that it would ever change. Feeling alone and gloomy, she escaped to her room as soon as they arrived home.

She pulled out her traveling bag and began to fill it with her belongings. Carefully, she packed her new dress they had picked up at the dressmakers. She hid the silver dollar coin in the folds of the dress. She smiled as she remembered that day she had spent with Robert. She had enjoyed her stay here except for the last week. She had felt like a prisoner, and she had not even been allowed to go outside and play with Jack.

Tomorrow she would take the train and leave to go back to her parent's farm in Mount Pleasant, Iowa. Emma's heart was filled with sadness. Mary had become like a sister to her, and Emma would miss their quiet conversations. These six weeks had flown by quickly and Emma wondered what it would be like to be in her father's house again. She was feeling a bit lost and realized she did not want to go home. Home to a room without her sister, Grace. Home to heartbreak and lonesomeness, where instead of four people there would only be three. She didn't know if she could watch again the pain in her mother's eyes and feel the sorrow that permeated their farmhouse. Perhaps the cook position wouldn't have been so bad, if it had gotten her out of her parent's home.

Then there was Robert. She didn't know exactly what to make of their acquaintance. He had given her no clues to what he thought of her. Yet he never failed to wait and wave at her in the morning before he went on his way to work, a gesture she found herself looking forward to each day.

She sat down on the bed and looked in her bag for a piece of paper and an envelope. She walked down the stairs to the front parlor and sat down at the desk. She dipped the quill pen into the ink and thought long and hard about what she wanted to say. Once the lines were written she stared at them for a moment, undecided, then pushed the paper into the envelope.

Mary walked into the room holding the baby and saw her sitting there.

"My dear you can't be writing your parents yet another letter. Surely it would not reach them before you arrive home?"

"No, Mary, I'm writing to a friend."

"Ah, you want to have a welcoming committee when you arrive home. Very smart to plan ahead."

Emma shook her head. "This friend does not live in Mount Pleasant." Emma turned and looked at her cousin. "I will miss you and the children."

Mary patted Emma's arm with her hand. "You'll always be welcome here."

Emma waited most of the evening until Mary and Charles had put the children to bed. She then slipped her coat on. Now that it was May, she hardly needed it. She carefully closed the door not to make a sound. She walked through the gate unto the road. She looked back to see if Mary was watching from the window, but Emma saw no one looking through the curtains. She walked briskly to Robert's house. She mounted the two steps to his porch. She bent down near his front door and slid the envelope under it. Robert would find it when he got home. She thought it only right that he should know that she was leaving.

TWELVE

GOING HOME

Charles had insisted that Emma travel on the Rock Island, Chicago train instead of the stagecoach. It was safer Charles said especially since she was traveling alone. Emma had learned Mary never went against her husband's wishes, and Emma was expected to follow suite. When Charles had come home one evening with a train ticket shortly after her visit to the dressmaker Emma knew her fate was sealed.

Emma had never travelled on a train before and felt a bit uneasy. When they arrived at the depot, there was a huge crowd milling around. They had to tunnel their way through the mass of humanity. Emma was jostled by warm bodies as she followed Charles. The closer they walked to the train, Emma realized what a huge steel monster it was. The black steel engine at the front of the train was cylindrical in shape with large wheels and attached to it was a series of many cars. The cars were different shapes and sizes. Emma could not see over the crowd to count how many there were. Emma was excited to see what the cars looked like inside.

"Hold tight to your traveling bag and be careful where you put it on the train. It's been known for dishonest people to take them." Charles said as they slowly walked toward the train. Emma's eyes widened in alarm, but she said never a word. "I wouldn't put it in the baggage car since you have only the one bag. Put it on the shelf above your head after you find a seat. We best hurry, the seats are not reserved."

They finally got to the last car where the conductor stood, Emma handed him her ticket. The man studied her ticket. "You are in the coach car," he said, "not this Pullman car." He glanced at the crowd and at tiny Emma. He gave her his hand and helped her board the train. "It will be easier for you to reach the coach car if you walk through the Pullman car and the dining car. The coach cars are the next two, after them. One coach car is for men only and the other one is for the women and children. If you go any further you will be in the emigrant cars. The porter will show you the way." He nodded to the shorter man next to him. "This way Miss."

Emma gave Charles a quick hug and she mounted the stairs of the train and entered into a brand new world. Her eyes opened wide as she took in her surroundings. The Pullman car looked quite comfortable and plush. The chairs were padded with velvet seats and there were beds that could be pulled down from the ceiling. Small tables were available for writing or for playing games. A small bar was located at the end of the car where fine wines and liquor could be bought. She spied a spittoon in the corner, for man to spit in when they were chewing or smoking their tobacco. There was also wash rooms one for the men and one for the ladies.

The car was made from mahogany, black walnut and oak

wood. The floor was carpeted. They walked past the chairs and sleeping berths. The car could hold about twenty passengers. One of the beds had a person sleeping in it and she could hear his snoring. A cloth running from the ceiling to the floor separated the sleeping person from the rest of the travelers.

Emma wished that her cousin could have booked her a seat on the Pullman car, but Charles said the seats had already been reserved by other people.

The next car was the dining car where meals could be purchased for seventy-five cents. Several tables sat on each side of the car, with sofa-like chairs separating them. Charles said the food was quite good, and the chefs did a wonderful job. He and Mary had taken a trip by train to Burlington, Iowa, not long ago and had ordered dinner on the train.

Finally, the porter led her to the coach car where many women were already claiming their seats, pushing and shoving each other for the best chairs. Unlike the Pullman car, seats were not reserved in the coach car. The coach car was plain and did not have all the fancy luxury of the Pullman. It reminded Emma of what Noah's ark must have looked like in the Bible, a long narrow box with a flat roof. There were no beds, just chairs and a passage hall down the middle of the seats to allow people to move from one end of the car to another. Emma chose a seat near the stove. Even though it was May, temperatures during the day could still be chilly.

The chairs in the coach section were made of slats and some had wicker cushions. Some had hinged backs so you could adjust them if you wanted to sleep. She chose one of them. Mary had told her to wear the same traveling clothes she had worn when she first arrived on the stagecoach. After a few hours on the train her dress would become rumpled, and if some passenger was silly enough to open a window, her attire might get dusty from the smoke and cinders tossed out by the train's engine.

Emma placed her bag on the floor near her feet. Mary had also packed her a lunch of fresh fruit, cookies and a sandwich. Emma place this cloth bag and her purse in her lap.

The coach filled up quickly. An older lady about the same age as Emma's mother and wearing a fancy bonnet sat down next to her. The woman was plump and her face round like the moon. Her blue eyes shone brightly.

"Don't you just love traveling by train?"

"I never have," confessed Emma.

"Oh, you will enjoy it," continued the woman. "My youngest son was employed by the railroad to lay down the rails and I promised him I'd ride on it when it was finished. And so I have. I'm on my way home to Iowa City after visiting my sister in Council Bluffs. He made good wages. A dollar twenty-five a day while he worked for the railroad. He said the work was hard. At first he spent much of his pay in saloons and on hall girls. But later he wised up and sent much of his earnings to me to save so he could purchase some property of his own. He said most of the people he worked with on the railroad were new to this country, unlike our family who has been here for some time. He heard a lot of stories about foreign countries like Ireland, Germany and Norway from those workers who could speak English. His time with the railroad has been a great adventure."

This woman loved to talk and would not be quiet. She changed subjects without taking a breath, and before Emma could reply. She chattered on about her sister's family, described their house and the food and the activities they had done during her stay. Emma nodded in the right places and tried to act interested.

Emma was glad when the train started to move and she could turn away from the woman to look out the window. The train started with a jerk and the conductor blasted a horn to alert those nearby that they were moving. The train slowly increased its speed until Emma felt like she was riding on a runaway horse. Never had she been in a carriage that moved as fast as the train. She had read in the railroad brochure that trains could reach the speeds of forty to sixty miles per hour.

As the train rambled forward, she watched the buildings of Des Moines disappear from sight. The prairies of Iowa and the farm fields soon appeared. She saw men in the fields driving horses attached to plows, turning the soil over, readying it for planting. Furrows of dark dirt lined the hillside.

Emma's own father would be hard at work doing the same things on the days when the weather permitted it. They owned three work horses, Sam, Midge and Tut. Their horses were well-trained in the art of farm work. Her father could control them with voice commands. The word "gee" meant turn to the right, the word "haw" meant turn to the left and "whoa" meant stop.

Her mind soon wandered and she tried to imagine what Robert had thought when he had read her letter. Would he regret her leaving as much as she did?

Emma soon became tired of looking at the passing farmland and settled down to read a romance novel her cousin had given her. The author was a pastor of the first Presbyterian Church in Highland Falls, New York, and this was his first novel. Mary had told her it was quite good. The book had first appeared in the newspaper as a serial before being printed in book form.

℀

It had been a long couple of days. After work Robert had checked on a friend, William, who lost a leg in the war. He had spent the night at William's residence before returning to work the next day. Robert tried to go see his friend once or twice a week to lift his spirits. William had a hard time making a living with a wooden leg, and the ghosts of the war haunted him worse than they did Robert. Some people called William crazy, but Robert knew better. William was often saddened by his fate but did what he could to cope.

William had recently moved into the new Polk County Poor Farm located on the far north side of town in Saylor Township. The farm consisted of two hundred and eighty acres that the residents were asked to work to provide for their own food. It had a frame house three stories high, with a brick-walled cellar. The structure contained twenty-seven rooms with comfortable quarters for the thirty people who lived there, those people that society considered paupers, or insane.

William had moved there several months ago and for the first time since the war was living with other people. Robert discovered that William was faring rather well there and that some of his odd behaviors were going away. He had found William in good spirits, smiling and laughing. The Directors of the farm, J. C. and his wife, had put his friend to work. He helped care for the chickens and gathered the eggs. Having a purpose in life helped William to keep his mind off his troubles, and he had even gained on a little weight.

Most people would think living at the Poor Farm a disgrace and humbling experience, but it had proved the opposite for his William. He no longer had to live in the out of doors or in the poorest housing situations. William had an independent spirit, and it had taken Robert several months to convince him to move there. The Director of the farm had suggested that William look into getting a pension for his service in the Civil War, for he had heard many invalid soldiers of the war of 1812 had received help through the U.S. Pension Office. William and Robert had talked about this subject, but William was not convinced he wanted to do this.

Robert was late when he returned home. He was glad that spring had come and the sun shone longer in the evening. He now had light when he made his journey home from work, and he no longer feared that some person might attack him. The war had taught him to be alert for any danger, and he could not control his apprehension when the night fell.

Robert put his horse in the stable and gave him a rubdown with some bushes. He then walked to his house in the fading light. When he opened the door, his foot stepped on something and he felt it slip beneath him. Robert caught his balance, then lit the kerosene lamp and investigated what he had stepped on. It was a small envelope now covered with his dirty foot print. Robert found this strange. Why would someone slip it under his door instead of using the postal service? He took the envelope, rubbed it on his pants to remove the dirt, and sat down on a chair in his semi-dark parlor. He put the lamp on the small table next to the chair so he could read better. Carefully he opened the envelope and a letter spilled out onto his lap. He opened the letter and held it to the light.

The writer had fine penmanship, neat and flowing. It was obvious the author of the letter had spent some time in school. He read the note twice, then stared into space. His emotions raged within him, the words etched in his mind.

Dear Robert:

By the time you receive this letter I will be on a train back to my home in Mount Pleasant, Iowa. My stay with my cousin, Mary, has come to an end. I wanted you to know I will no longer be in the window each morning and I did not want you to worry. You will still be in my thoughts and I promise to say a prayer for you each day that you will be strong and stay well. Thank you for showing me and telling about the town of Des Moines. It will be a memory that I will cherish. I enjoyed our conversations.

Sincerely,
Emma Edward

Robert looked down again at the letter and read it several times, trying to read between the lines what Emma meant about saying a prayer for him. Was it just a kind gesture or did it mean something more?

He felt a deep sadness come over him, and loneliness overwhelmed him. He had not realized how much seeing her each morning in the window had meant to him. He was not sure what to do with the feelings. The strength of them shook him, for he had never felt such emotions for another human being. In war he had felt grief for his fallen friends and soldiers, but he had never felt this pain in his heart.

The darkness and the coldness of his house reflected how he felt. He knew not what to do. He turned off the lamp and walked quickly to his bed. Perhaps sleep could dampen these feelings into forgetfulness.

THIRTEEN

HER PARENTS' FARM

Her brother Jonah picked Emma up in his wagon at the train station in Iowa City. Instead of taking two days to cross the Iowa prairies in a stagecoach, the train had arrived the same day. Emma had marveled how quickly her trip had been. She barely had time to eat the sandwich Mary had packed for her.

Jonah was three years older than she Emma and the youngest of her three brothers. But he seemed more worldly and much wiser than she. At age eighteen he had married the store-keeper's daughter and had helped her father ever since. It was as if he couldn't wait to grow up and be on his own. He said it was his sisters' fault. There were too many women in his family home, and perhaps he had been right. But now he had a little girl of his own and he spoiled her every chance he could.

Jonah helped her into his wagon and told her he had not had to wait long for the train. Figuring out when a train was to arrive and depart was often a difficult matter. The United States did not have a consistent clock system and different states and towns often had different times. This made little sense to Emma, but Mary had explained the clock problem to Emma one evening when they were discussing her traveling adventures. Jonah tossed Emma's bag into the wagon and they were off.

"How are mother and father?" Emma asked. She wanted to be prepared when she arrived home. Would she be returning to a house of sadness and gloom?

"Better," Jonah said, not one for words. "You'll find out soon enough."

The speed of the wagon horses seemed incredibly slow after having been on the train. Emma passed the time talking to her brother of what had been happening in Mount Pleasant since she had left and looking at the scenery along the road. The sun soon disappeared behind the horizon in a stunning sunset of purple, gold and pink. Darkness overtook them, and they completed the last leg of their journey by the light of the moon.

Her parents' house was small compared to her cousin Mary's and looked dreary and isolated when they arrived at their destination. However, a lamp glowed in the window, welcoming her home.

Jonah helped Emma down from the wagon, then unhitched the weary horses and led them to the barn. He had decided to spend the night at the farm instead of returning to his house in town.

Emma stretched her arms high above her head, for she was stiff, dirty and tired from her travels. It took a few minutes for her legs to loosen up before she could walk to the house. She walked up the porch and entered into the dark home. Her father greeted her with a hello and a quick hug.

"Your mother's gone to bed, but I told her I would stay up until you arrived."

Her father had a strong English accent that he had not lost even though he had lived in America for many years. His hands were large and callused from hard work in the fields, and he had developed a rounded belly that stuck out from his lean frame.

Emma hugged her father back, then went and sat down by the stove to warm up. When it had turned to night on their journey to the farm, a brisk wind started to blow, and it had chilled Emma to the bone.

Emma could barely see the furniture in the room, but she knew exactly what was in the room. She had lived in this house for twelve years and had watched her brothers and father build it. She had been eight years old when her family had crossed the ocean from England. She barely remembered living there. Iowa was all she had known.

Her father brought her some warm soup her mother had left for her. She was so tired from her travels, she barely had strength to eat it.

"How did you like riding on the train?" her father asked with interest. He had seen the great machines from a distance, but had never been on one.

"It is very fast," Emma said, "but the seats are uncomfortable after you sit on them a while. The car swayed a bit when it moved, like a baby in a cradle. For the most part I enjoyed the ride and looking out the window. I met many interesting people. It was quite an adventure. You and mother will have to take a trip sometime."

Just then her brother walked in and he sat down and joined them in their meal. Emma thought her father's disposition had improved. He smiled instead of frowned. He even chuckled when she told him about a little boy on the train who refused to be still and had crawled up onto her lap. He then pulled her hair. She pulled his hair back. That made him yell and his mother came and recused her from any more torture. After the story ended she got up and went to bed.

❧

Emma woke up with a jerk. For a moment she knew not where she was. She rubbed the sleep from her eyes and looked around the room. She was not at Mary's house but in her own room on her father's farm. This room was tiny compared to the one she had occupied the last six weeks. Someday she dreamed she would have a fine house like her cousin's.

She climbed out of bed and out of habit searched for a window to stand beside. But her bedroom had not a window. Her room was more like a loft than a separate room. She blinked her eyes, trying to hide her sense of disappointment. She scolded herself for her silliness.

She looked down at the tiny bed next to her own, the bed where her sister, Grace, should have been. Laying on the bed was the most colorful quilt she had ever seen. She walked to the other bed to study the quilt more closely. The crazy patterned quilt was not the type of quilt her mother commonly made. The crazy quilt pattern had just become popular and had no organized pattern.

Her mother saved every scrap of material she could from making dresses, aprons, and shirts, then made them into quilts. But in this quilt she had used frilly, colorful, expensive material like silk and velvet. She had sown the material together in odd shapes and varied sizes. But even though the shapes were random sizes, her mother had somehow placed the material together in such a way that the colors blended into a pleasing orchestra to the eye.

Emma ran her hand over the quilt. Slowly she came to realize that some of the colorful shapes had come from the special-occasion dress her sister had always worn. The other material was from Grace's hope chest. When Grace would go to her brother's store she would ask him and his wife for any scrapes of material that were two small to sell. She picked out only those fabrics that were the most expensive. She would then hide them in her special hope chest. She would pull them out occasionally to show Emma and tell her made up stories about people who wore them. It was a harmless way to pass the time in the winter, and Grace had been a great storyteller. Emma had encouraged her to write down the stories but she never did.

Memories of Grace danced in her head. Grace had been her primary companion growing up. Their temperaments could not have been more different. Grace had been named well. She had been an obedient child and kind to everyone. Over the years she had brought into their house a collection of hurt rabbits, birds, and dogs and nursed them back to health.

Her kindness also extended to people. She was the first to speak to a classmate who wore glasses and to the boy who walked with a limp. Emma, on the other hand, was strong–willed, and her opinions often clashed with her parents. Grace would be the peacemaker and calm everyone down when raised voices filled their home. Grace had wisdom beyond her thirteen years and understood Emma better than her parents did.

Emma put on her clothes and went down the stairs. She found her mother in the kitchen. Her mother was a short, round woman. After birthing five children, her figure had never returned to its slim, youthful shape. But she was nimble on her feet and she moved around the room like a dancer at a ball.

She turned from the stove where she had been cooking when she heard Emma's footsteps. She eyes shone with pleasure at the sight of her daughter.

"I am glad you're home. I missed you. This house seems too quiet with all of my children gone."

Emma was startled at how bright her mother looked. When she had left in March, her mother's face had been etched in pain and sorrow. It also appeared that her mother had regained the weight she had lost due to her sorrow.

"You're looking wonderful, Mother. What has transpired to lift your mood?"

Her mother laughed. "Sit down, child, and I will tell you a most interesting tale." She explained that with Emma gone, she and her husband had argued continuously about little things until both had hurt feelings. It was as if they were taking their sorrow over Grace out on each other. One day after a heated disagreement, she had left their house in a fury and walked to the next farm in search of consolation. Her husband was so filled with anger at his misfortune of losing two children that she feared for his sanity. She talked to Granny May about her troubles and her pain. Granny May was eighty years old and listened to her tale in quiet solitude.

"Each person grieves in their own way," the old woman said. "Let your husband work out his sorrow in his way. It may take many months for him to recover from Grace's death. What you need is a project to stay busy until he has made peace with what has happened." Granny May then placed in her hand scraps of material. "Make a memorial quilt for your dead daughter. It will be good for both of you."

"While I lingered there," Mother continue her story, "a spring rain storm had set upon us and Granny May refused to let me walk back home. The next morning after the storm had passed, I went home to find your father scared and sick. He had spent the night searching for me and feared I had lost my way. He was crying when I entered the house, his face in his hands, begging for me to come home safe. I knew then that he was praying to a greater power. When I knelt beside him and held him in my arms, he clung to me and I helped him to bed.

"We never spoke again of that terrible day, but it changed us. We both in our hearts realized we still had something to live for, each other. We spent the rest of the time you were gone in warm companionship, never uttering a cross word to each other, although at times we still grieved for Grace.

"I found Grace's hope chest and used her material to make the quilt. The quilt reminded me of her every time I worked on it. She always had a bright, joyful spirit, like the bright, beautiful colors in the quilt. Always remember Emma, misfortune can either break you or teach you a lesson." Her mother placed the boxes of scraps left over from the quilt in Emma's hands. "Make one for yourself."

"I don't know how," Emma replied.

"I will teach you how," her mother said.

They spread the pieces of material out on the kitchen table and they talked about a design for the quilt. Emma chose a simple design. Four square blocks of colorful material about one-inch-wide were sewed together to form one big block. She then sewed white material around the big block, making a two-inch border. The big blocks would then be sown together.

Grace would have laughed at her plain design, but it made complete sense to Emma. As she and her mother cut and hand sewed the small blocks together, they talked of all the events that had happened in the last six weeks that they had been apart. Emma told her mother everything except about Robert. She was afraid that her mother would not approve of Robert.

FOURTEEN

REPLY

Several weeks later, Emma had just finished planting the last row of beans in the garden when her mother appeared walking towards her from the back of the house.

"Here's a letter for you." She placed the letter in Emma's hand. "Cousin Mary's handwriting seems to have gotten worse than the last time she wrote, or perhaps it from her husband Charles. They're the only people we know in Des Moines."

Emma looked at the letter, and her breath caught in her throat. She knew both Mary's and Charles' handwriting. This letter was not from them. Perhaps it was from one of the school directors she had written to just last week to see if they had any teacher openings, or perhaps . . . Something told her that this letter was important, and for a moment she was afraid to read its contents.

"Aren't you going to open it, or are you just going to look at it all day?"

Emma hadn't realized she had been standing like a statue staring at the letter for many minutes until her mother spoke again. Emma swallowed hard before she spoke.

"I have dirt on my hands. I would like to wash up first before reading it."

Her mother nodded. Emma walked to the house. Her mother followed her. After she washed up, she sat in a chair in the parlor and studied the envelope. The envelope was slightly crumpled as if it had been in a person's pocket for some time, or perhaps the postal service had caused the damage.

She smoothed the paper under her fingers to straighten it out. She then took a knife and opened one end. Carefully, she removed the paper that was hidden inside. The letter had the same sprawling handwriting. It was not easy to decipher, and it took Emma several minutes to read.

Dear Emma:

I received your letter and was surprised at your sudden departure. It sent me into a state of melancholy. I could not sleep. I have thought of you many times in the last few weeks especially at the break of day. This has prompted me to write. I would like to continue our friendship and ask your permission to correspond with you. Please reply at your earliest convenience to tell me if this is agreeable with you.

Robert Harding

Emma's hand trembled with excitement. She had a hard time believing that Robert had really written to her. It felt like a dream. She had hoped that he would write her. She even had prayed that he would, but she never truly believed that he would. Just this week Emma had given up that he would write her and tried not to be disappointed because he had not. Now before her, all her dreams had come true and she wanted to squeal in delight. She somehow kept her feelings trapped in her body and instead just smiled.

"Mary must have had something good to say," her mother remarked. "You are beaming."

Emma looked up at her mother and became tongue-tied. She wanted to tell her the truth, but something inside told her not to. She searched for a solution and decided on a half a truth instead.

"It's not from Mary, but from her neighbor that lives next door to her. We became good friends while I was in Des Moines, and we decided to continue our friendship through letters."

Yes, she would write Robert back.

"That's wonderful Emma. You cannot have too many friends."

Emma stood up quickly and walked to her room. She did not want her mother asking more questions about her letter, for she knew not how she would answer them. The letter's words echoed in her head as she mounted the stairs. She sat on her bed and read the letter again. He had thought of her. Surely that was a sign of his affection for her. While she had been at Mary's, he had never faltered in their morning routine, and she had hoped his attention meant something more. But she was unsure what it really meant. She was still unsure, but she was full of hope.

She sat down at her desk and began to write. She told him about her ride on the train and about the little boy that pulled her hair. She told him that her parents were well and that she was busy planting seeds in the garden. She ended the letter that she would be pleased to write to him. She posted the letter herself when she went to town the following day.

As she went about her chores the next week, her mind often became cluttered with thoughts of Robert. She would see his face, his house, and wondered if his garden fruit trees were blooming. She found herself smiling and humming when these thoughts appeared. Her chores of gathering eggs from the hens and making butter with the milk churn no longer seemed burdensome but a time to reflect and hope another letter would soon appear.

Robert did not disappointment her, and she guessed he must have sat down with ink and a quill the moment he received her reply. Before the week had commenced she received yet another letter from him, this one much longer than the first one.

He wrote of visiting his friend William at the poor farm. William, he explained, was his best friend. He was several years older than Robert and had helped him find work when he had first come to live in Des Moines. They also had hunted wild turkey and pheasants when they needed food. William had taught Robert how to shoot and how to cook the birds.

But that all changed at Shiloh. William too had volunteered to serve. As they had retreated back to the road later called the "Hornet Nest," he had been shot several times in his leg. Robert had tied a scarf around William's leg to stop the bleeding. They went on fighting until the end of the battle. The Union doctors could not save William's leg. To save his life, they had amputated his leg below the knee.

William struggled from then on and lived a miserable life. He picked up work where he could, but there was not much demand for a man with a wooden leg. His friend was proud and he would not beg for food. He lived off the land in a tent on the edge of town. He saved his money, what little of it there was, for housing in the winter time. Robert never knew exactly where William might camp, for he moved frequently. Many a night he had to search for William's campfire. Robert had convinced him to go to the new poor house farm to live this year during the winter, and William had found it much to his liking. He had found a place to call home.

"You asked why I returned home late at night and that is why. I often go to see my friend William."

He hoped Emma could one day meet his friend, for William was a courageous man.

It took Emma an hour or more to read Robert's letter. He wrote with proper grammar, but his handwriting was poor. It rambled along on the paper, with few loops on circle letters and slanted heavily toward the right.

Once she figured out what he was telling her, she would read the letter again and again to make sure she had not misinterpreted any of the words. She thought it would become easier after she became familiar with his handwriting, but it was not any easier as more letters arrived. She teased him about his handwriting once, saying his letters always kept her in suspense like a puzzle, until the end of them when she had figured out all his words.

She learned much about Robert through his letters. He told her about parents who still lived in Ohio and how he had moved to Iowa with his sister, Lena, and her husband, George Anderson, many years ago. They had heard of the fine land in Iowa. They traveled forty-five days in a wagon to reach their new home.

He wrote fondly of the man that had bought him his first

carpentry tools and taught him how to build a barn, then a house, then a building. He talked of everyday things that happened, about the berries and apples that had ripened in his garden. Emma chuckled when he wrote that he saw Jack one day in Charles' yard, chasing rabbits.

She in return wrote him stories of her life on the farm.

"I feel like an old woman," she wrote in June, "like one of those corn plants that dried up because there was no rain. The heat has made me listless. I can find no place that is cool. Even the shade under the trees is warm. One night I tried sleeping out on the porch, but the bugs drove me inside."

In an August letter, she told him she celebrated her nineteenth birthday.

"I look around me and I wonder if my life will ever count for anything. If my parents were only more well-off, I would take more classes at the College here in town. My friend Bella took classes there while the Civil War raged and graduated valedictorian of her class. She married a professor at the college. She is active in the women's suffrage movement. Her life seems very exciting, while mine is dull. We talk often of her ambition, and she has loaned me a few of her schoolbooks to encourage me."

Two weeks later, she sadly penned him that she would not be returning to Des Moines any time soon. No one was interested in hiring her as a teacher.

Her mother noticed that the letters from Robert were stacking up in her room. One evening while they were quilting, she said, "Your friend seems to be quite a writer. Perhaps she wants to be a newspaper editor or a novelist."

Emma giggled and she nicked her finger with her needle, causing it to bleed. She put her finger in her mouth to lick off the blood and waited for it to stop the flow. She smiled at her mother in the dim light of the candle.

"No, my friend is not writer but a carpenter. I must confess I have kept you in the dark these past few months, for I knew not what to make of our correspondence. The writer of those letters is Robert Harding, the man that lives next to Mary."

Emma's mother put down her quilt piece and looked fondly at her daughter. "Ah, a young man has finally taken a liking to you. I wondered when that would happen."

"We have become good friends," agreed Emma. She went back to her quilting and said no more. Robert never said what he thought of her. He seemed content to have her as a friend. Emma had to admit to herself that she felt differently. His words seemed to have lured her like bait in a trap to feel much more. Her heart was overflowing with kind feelings toward Robert, and she wanted to tell him of her devotion. She was afraid to put her feelings into words. She feared he would turn away and she would never hear from him again.

Robert's letter came with the mail. She went quickly to her bedroom loft and laid upon her bed. She ripped the letter open. She noticed something different about it immediately. His handwriting had improved.

Dear Emma:

In less than a month the Allen's wonderful mansion will be finished and we have only the touch up work in the inside to keep us busy. I will soon be out of a job but that is not uncommon for carpenters. The winter weather makes it difficult to start a new structure. I usually use the extra time to make wooden chairs at my residence. I have had much success in selling them to the dealer of furniture in town. With the extra time I have found myself with, I have taken your advice and took a class to improve my handwriting so you do not have to struggle with my words. The class was taught by a Miss Jones, a friendly woman who praised my efforts to better myself. We have become good friends and even shared a meal together. I hope our friendship will continue because I have become quite fond of her.

Emma threw down Robert's letter and stomped around the small room. Anger rose up inside her like a flame that touches dry wood. Robert was fond of Miss Jones, was he? He wanted their friendship to continue. Images of a blond-haired beauty with sparkling blue eyes and a slim figure leaped to her mind. Had he found himself a wife?

Emma dashed to find a sheet of paper and in haste penned a burning reply to Robert.

Dear Robert:

I have received your letter and was taken by surprise that you had found another female companion to spend your time with. You have never told me how you feel about me, but I had drawn conclusions of my own from our long correspondence that we were more than just friends. My heart has betrayed me and given itself to you. It is broken in two to learn that you have found dear another woman. This will be my last letter to you, for I cannot bear to write to you again.

Emma

With haste, she put the letter in the envelope and decided that she must go to town. She hitched up old Nellie, a gentle sorrel horse that her father no longer used in the fields. She drove herself to town and took her letter to the post office. She then went to see her brother at the store. He was pleased to see her, and they talked of many things.

"Tell mother we just received two sewing machines. We can sell them on payment. I know she had been wanting one. Perhaps she and father can come look at them, and we can figure out a way she can own one."

"Ah, you are always a salesman, Jonah. I will tell her."

With that, Emma left. Her heart burst on the way home. She felt the pain of loss once again. This hurt was different than the one she had when she had lost Grace. This pain stung like a knife that made a cut on the skin. The pain bled like blood. She shook her head and sighed. Tears fell from her eyes. She wiped them away with her hands.

Stop it, she told herself. She must stop the pain. She tried to think of other things. She lifted her head and saw the sun burning brightly in the sky. She would live through this misfortune. She had lived through worse. She would be strong.

∽

Emma went to bed early that night. She told her mother that she was weary from her trip to town. She threw herself upon the bed and tried not to think, but words filled her head. Had she been too hasty with her reply to Robert? Had her heart ruled her head? Had she ruined the best thing that had come into her life?

She tried to imagine what Robert would think when he got her letter. Would he be sad or would he be glad to be rid of her now that he had found Miss Jones?

She rolled around all night and sleep refused to come. Her bed felt hard and uncomfortable. She tossed and turned. She pounded her fists on the bed. What had she done? She must have fallen asleep late in the night, for when she next opened her eyes the dawn had come. She dressed quickly and went to eat breakfast with her mother.

The days passed in endless succession, each the same as the last. Emma wilted in the summer heat. She carried water from the creek that ran past their pasture and watered the garden every day. Her father wished he could do the same with his fields. He worried that if they did not have rain soon, the crops would be ruined.

The ground and crops seemed like Emma's heart, burnt and in need of refreshment. The grass started to turn brown. Emma waited anxiously for a reply from Robert. She waited ten days. No letter came. She accepted her fate.

And then it rained. The storm came in the afternoon, and the lightening lit up the gray cloudy sky. Rain sounded like the thunder of a hundred horses' hooves hitting the roof of their home. As the water refreshed the earth, so did the rain refresh Emma.

FIFTEEN

THE HARVEST

"Hurry, Emma! Stack the plates on the table and don't forget the silverware. The thresher men will be coming in for lunch very soon."

Emma nodded and ran to do her mother's bidding. They had been hard at work for two days preparing to feed twelve hungry men that came with the horse-drawn threshing machine. Her father did not own such a machine, but his neighbor did. The machine made quick work of separating the grain from the heads, separating the straw by a blower, and it removed the chaff from the grain in a single operation. The machine was used on the wheat, rye and oats that were growing in their fields.

The men gathered together with the machine for a hard day's labor. Emma and her mother worked just as hard. Women in the community tried to outdo each other and hoped the thresher men would find their cooking the best of them all.

Her mother had decided to roast a turkey on a spit over an open fire outdoors while Emma cooked squash, Indian pudding, and biscuits on the stove inside. Sweat ran down Emma's face, and she wiped it away with a wet towel. The house was hot with all her cooking. Her back and feet hurt from standing up on them all day.

She placed the dishes and cups on the table. She had filled several pitchers with water for the men to drink. Emma looked out the window and could see the men walking towards the house. They, too, looked hot and tired from their labors. Many of them washed their hands and face under the water pump outside.

Her sister-in-law, Katherine, walked in the door with a basket of food in her arms. Her husband, David, Emma's oldest brother, was helping the thresher team. Katherine placed three homemade pies along with pickles and jams on the table.

"Are we ready?" she asked. "The men are here."

"I have cut the meat," Emma's mother said and placed two large platters piled high with slices of turkey in the center of the table. Just then her husband appeared, leading the parade of men through the house.

Their house was not big enough for all the men to eat inside. They took their turns heaping their plates with food, then went outside to sit on the ground under the shade of the trees. Emma could hear their voices humming like a bird's song. After all the men were seated, she took a pitcher of water and walked around them, refilling their cups.

"Emma, it is good to see you and thank you for the fine dinner you have prepared," the man with the sunburned face said. His blue eyes twinkled and his mouth held a wide smile.

"Why, Abe Nelson, it is nice of you to say so."

This man lived to the south of their farm, and his father owned the thresher machine. Abe was a several years older than Emma but appeared years younger. He was short, just a few inches taller than Emma, and small-boned and thin.

Rumors had it that he had gone out west in search of adventure and had just recently returned a wiser but poorer man. He had been boasting to anyone that would listen to him in the saloons about all the places he had been and things that he had done. He said he was looking for a wife and had not yet settled his attention on just one. He seemed to want to try out the whole henhouse before he made his pick, thought Emma.

Abe lifted his empty cup toward her, and Emma poured him some water from the pitcher. His wide smile and glowing eyes made Emma uncomfortable. She blushed red as he looked at her from the tip of her head to the soles of her shoes. He seemed to like what he saw.

"Your brother, David, told me you are still unmarried. Perhaps I should come courting?"

Emma stared down at the man and shook her head. Abe's comment seemed forward.

"My brother likes to think I am unhappy, but I am not. I have plenty to do. And I don't think Caroline would take kindly to the notion. It's best you stay with her."

Abe frowned and looked away, clearly getting her message that she was not interested. Caroline, a sturdy, plain woman, had been seen on many occasions in his company. Caroline, a woman of few morals, was often the talk of the town. If Abe liked such a woman, he was not the man for Emma, even though his compliment about her cooking had brightened her spirits. Perhaps there was hope yet that one day she would marry.

Emma walked away and chatted with some of the older men who were her father's age and brought them more biscuits or a piece of pie from the house. The time went quickly, and the men rose and returned to the fields. Soon the women were left with dirty dishes and the few remains of the dinner. The men had eaten it all.

Emma, her mother, and her sister-in-law sat on the porch and rested. They talked quietly among themselves and watched Billie, Emma's nephew, play in the yard.

"It doesn't seem right that a meal takes days to prepare and only a short time to eat," Emma said. She was tired and felt like she could sleep for a week after this day was over.

Her mother told the two other women stories about how they used to harvest the fields before the horse-drawn threshing machine. It had been a long and laborious task cutting the wheat and rye with hand flails, then beating the plants to separate seeds.

That is why they grew more wheat, oats and rye instead of corn. The threshing machine could not be used on corn. Corn would still be harvested by hand later in the year. The men would come back later and chop down the corn stalks one at a time. They would then stack them in the fields to dry. The shocks would look like a hundred teepees in the field. Once dried they were loaded into a wagon and taken to their homestead to remove the corn from the stalks. Emma and her mother would help with the removal of the corn. Emma's father raised little corn, just enough to feed the horses and other livestock.

Once the women were done, they returned to the task of cleaning up. Emma had never seen so many dirty dishes.

SIXTEEN

THE SURPRISE

A few days later, Emma opened the door to their house and was shocked to see Robert standing on the porch. She barely had sense enough to say hello. She stood still, like a deer caught in the moonlight, stiff and alert, her eyes wide open and staring, unable to believe what she saw. They stared at each other not saying a word.

Robert shuffled his weight from foot to foot, unable to read her expression, whether she was pleased to see him or not. Her father, concerned by the silence, came to her rescue and stood next to her. Father, too, was surprised at the muscular giant at his door. Robert's six-foot-tall frame towered over Emma's father's head by four inches. Emma had not realized how short her father was until that moment. He had always seemed tall to her.

Robert held out his hand in greeting.

"I'm Robert Harding, a friend of Emma's. I've come to speak with her."

"Friend." The word echoed in Emma's head. If they were only friends, why had he come?

Father turned to Emma. He saw the look of confusion on her face. Emma quickly hid her discontent and smiled.

"Robert lives next to Cousin Mary. I met him on my trip there. We have been communicating by letters for some time."

"Ah, that friend that writes to you," Father said as he turned his head to study Robert again.

"How did you know? I get the mail most days and took his letters out before I gave the rest to Mother."

Father led the way through their small sitting room.

"I know most everything that concerns my household." He winked at Emma. "Besides, my wife told me about the letters."

Emma's mouth fell open in surprise.

"Won't you come in and take a seat." Father led Robert into the large kitchen that also served as the parlor. It held an eating table with six chairs, a stove and a sofa chair that Father relaxed in at night, and Mother's rocking chair. The room was connected to her parent's bedroom. The only other room on the first floor was for storage where they kept canned vegetables, wood, and other household necessities. Mother offered him a drink of iced tea, which Robert accepted. They all sat down and an awkward silence came upon them.

Father said, "Perhaps you can tell me what has caused you to come to our home on a visit?"

Father and Mother waited for Robert to speak. Emma clutched her hands in her lap and stared at him with interest, her heart beating fiercely in her chest, and she was sure everyone in the room could hear it. Robert's eyes met Emma's and the edges of his mouth turned up slightly, although he did not smile. Emma had seen this action before when Robert was amused. She wondered what he found funny and could not help but grin back at him.

At last he spoke, his voice steady and firm.

"I believe Emma misinterpreted my last letter, and I felt the need to set things right in person."

"Hmm," Father said. "I'm sure Emma will be glad to talk to you about it in private. But first, I would like to know more about you."

Robert obliged. Father then talked with Robert for over an hour. Father and Robert had many things in common, Robert being a carpenter and a farmer's son. Emma's father had been a millwright when he lived in England. He and Robert talked about the trades and the recent harvest. Emma soon became bored with the conversation.

Robert spied her impatience.

"I would very much like to take a walk with your daughter. I have a need for some fresh air."

Father nodded his approval. Emma rose from her chair at the table and Robert stood up as well.

"I could show you the farm," she said. "It is a very nice farm."

They headed out the doors, and Emma led him away from the house down a path toward the barns.

"Father and Mother started to raise chickens last year, and it has been quite profitable for them. Mother trades the eggs in town for flour and sugar and other things she needs. Some of the chickens she butchers for meat."

They stopped by the chicken coop and watched the flock of chickens dig in the dirt. Robert looked at the chickens, then at Emma. Emma looked back at him and saw a gleam in his eye. She turned away, caught off guard.

"Over there," she said, pointing, "is the garden I have written you about." The vegetables had come up, and tomatoes, cucumbers, and squash hung on the vines.

"It is a fine garden, but that is not why I have come."

Emma moved away from him and could not look him in the face.

"You have come to tell me about Miss Jones. You like her very much . . ." Emma paused and whispered, "I understand that she would not like you writing me. I will miss our friendship."

Robert's mouth turned up a bit more.

"I did not know until your last letter, when you expressed in no uncertain terms your distress about my acquaintance with Miss Jones, that . . ."

"You spoke of her in glowing terms." Emma raised her eyebrows and turned to look at him with a frown on her face. "It caused me pain." She bowed her head, not wanting him to see the tears that glistened in her eyes.

"I never meant to cause you discomfort, nor was I aware how much pleasure you took in my letters. In fact, I was quite pleased to discover that your affection for me matches mine for you."

Emma abruptly ran to Robert and grabbed onto his arms.

"You are teasing me."

Robert looked into her startled eyes.

"No, Miss, I am not, and it saddens me that we are apart. I look each morning at your cousin's second-floor window and wish you were still there to wave at me. If you are willing, I would like to ask your father for your hand in marriage. But before you say anything, I must tell you, Emma, that I am not a rich man and if you accept my proposal, our life may not be easy. But I will promise you that I will always work hard to provide for you and be loyal to you. And God willing, we will always have a roof over our heads and food on our table."

"I will," she said.

"What?"

"I will gladly become your wife."

Robert pulled Emma into his arms, bent his head and kissed her gently on the lips. Emma pulled her head away and looked him in the eyes.

"That was very fine, Mr. Harding, and I would very much like to try that again."

She leaned into him and lifted her face to meet his lips. Robert kissed her once again, this time long and with passionate yearning. Emma rose on her toes and placed her hands around his head and shoulders and let her body melt into his. They kissed until her heart beat wildly within her chest and her body pulsed with desire. Emma's family dog, Blackie, barked and they pulled away. Emma looked around and blushed. Her six-year-old nephew, Billy, who had been staying with her folks, stared at them.

"What you're doing?" the small blonde-haired boy asked.

"Never you mind, Billy, what are you doing?" Emma said.

Billy giggled. He put his hands to his mouth and laughed some more, his face as red as Emma's blushing cheeks.

"You're kissing." He wrinkled his nose and giggled some more. "Don't look like much fun."

Robert walked over to the little boy and knelt down until his face was level with the youngster.

"I like your aunt. And she likes me. Sometimes folks kiss each other when they like each other."

Billy looked into Robert eyes. "I know. I've seen Ma and Pa

do it. But I don't like it when they kiss me." His top lip came out in a pout.

"I didn't like it either when I was your age. It's ok. It's just something grownups do."

Billy nodded, losing interest in the whole event. "Grandma wanted me to get you. Dinner is ready."

They walked back to the house, Emma's hand wrapped around Robert's elbow, her body leaned into his side. Billy led the way.

"Where did he come from?"

"He was in the yard back of the house. He and the dog like to go exploring in the woods."

Robert turned his head to look at Emma.

"The truth is that I want you for my wife, and wish not to be apart from you much longer. I believe fall would be a fine time for us to wed before the snow makes traveling difficult. It is also a time when I could spend much more time with you and we could learn each other's ways. For come spring, I already have several construction jobs lined up, and I might not be much at the house except to sleep. It is good that I live near Mary, for she will be a good neighbor for you."

Emma's head was spinning. It was happening all too fast. Yet she could see Robert's logic. She thought she might faint, so filled with joy was her being. But what would her parents say? She had only been home a short while, and her father had just learned of Robert. Might he be like Charles and think Robert strange?

SEVENTEEN

UNWELCOME GUESTS

Robert put another piece of wood in the fireplace and sat down on the wood chair he had made several years ago. He smiled to himself as he stared into the burning fire. Its flame burned just as bright as his love for Emma. Emma had been staying at Cousin Mary's house this past month at her father's request. He had suggested that Robert court Emma for a month and then if they were still of the same mind to wed, they could so in October. Mary Cooper had consented to the plan.

Robert had spent most evenings at the Cooper's. He had attended church with Emma on Sunday, although he still had doubts about God's existence. He had taken Emma and Charles to meet his friend, William. In a week the month would be over. Time had flown quickly and he was even surer of his decision. Emma had suggested they talk to the preacher after the service this weekend about when they could have their wedding. Her |eyes sparkled with delight as she said these words, and he had agreed.

Suddenly his thoughts were interrupted when he heard a pounding on his door. He walked to it and pulled it open. There stood his sister, Lena, tall and thin. She wore a shabby brown coat and a dirty bonnet. Her long black hair was braided and the one long strand fell against her shoulder. A wisp of a girl half her mother's size hid herself behind the woman.

It took Robert several minutes to recognize his sister. It had been five years since he had heard from or seen his sibling. Then she had been a beautiful woman. Today she looked alarming, haggard and sickly.

"I need your help. Something dreadful has happened. We lost the farm and have nowhere to go. Can we stay with you?"

"Is George with you?"

The woman nodded. Robert looked over his sister's head out onto the street and saw a man clothed in a black coat near a wagon filled to overflowing with furniture, clothes, and other household items. George turned and looked at Robert. In his mouth, he smoked a cigar. His eyes were cold as steel. The fall wind chilled Robert as well as the two fugitives, causing them to shiver. He ushered them inside.

"What is this about?"

"It is a long, sad story. I will tell you later after Anna has gone to bed." Lena looked down at her daughter and placed a protective arm around her shoulders. "Please say we can stay. We have no other place to go."

Robert saw the fear in his sister's eyes and could not in good conscience turn her away.

"You can stay the night until we get this sorted out. If you're hungry, there is food in the kitchen. I will help George put the horse away." With that, he went to the closet and put on his coat and went outdoors.

Robert walked to the cart in the street. He was not pleased.

What had George done to cause such distress in his sister? He approached the man with caution, for he knew of George's temper that could flare up in an instant.

George had treated Lena poorly at times while Robert had lived with them many years ago. George would cuss and yell at her, but he had never been a violent man, just one with a poor temperament.

When Robert had been seventeen, he had pointed this fact out to George when he was fussing at Lena. Robert had defended Lena in an argument and had stood between them. Robert was skinny in those day and built small, like any youth of that age. He had been no match for George, a full grown man hardened by the labor on the land. George had taken him by the arms and thrown him bodily out of his home without even a spare set of clothes and told him never to come back. Lena had found Robert in the barn the next day, hiding. She had prepared a bundle of his belongings and given him a few coins.

"I cannot make him change his mind, Robert. You must go," she had told him. "I wish you well. Write me when you are settled."

At first he had written her, because he was lonely, but after the war, he had discontinued writing to her.

Robert remembered that day as if it was yesterday and he still had some fear of the man. Once near the horse, Robert inquired, "What is going on George? Do tell me!"

George turned with a scowl on his face. The years had been kind to the man, his face still handsome although his body now was overgrown with a fat belly, which he hid within an overcoat. But Robert had grown taller in the past years and now stood above this man. Robert straightened to his full height and demanded an answer.

George took the cigar from his mouth and studied Robert. He was not pleased with what he saw, for he knew he could no longer push Robert round.

"We fell on hard times. I did what I could to keep them fed. Lena wanted to come here and start anew. If you could house us until I find a job and locate a few rooms, she would appreciate it. She is not much for camping out and winter is coming on."

Robert did not believe a word George said. There must be more to the story. They had owned a fine farm in Dubuque, Iowa, with many acres. It had been profitable when Robert was there. Why would they leave it behind?

"Besides you owe us," George added. "You know you do."

The words burned in Robert's soul. His face hardened. He fought to control his feelings. George hadn't changed.

"The barn is this way. Be careful. The path is narrow."

He took hold of the horse's bridle and led the way. His stable was small, more of a shed with just room enough for his horse, Soldier, to seek shelter on the coldest day. Attached to it was a small corral. With two horses in it, it would be a tight fit.

He unhitched the horse while George seemed content to watch and smoke his cigar. The smell of it filled the air. Robert could tell the horse was thin and had been driven hard, for there was dried sweat amidst its winter hair. Once he had the horse unhitched, he brushed it. He glanced at George, who leaned against the shed, unconcerned.

Robert said nothing, but inside anger boiled. In the war he had learned to care for his horse, for the animal was often the margin between life and death. The two men walked to the house, the sun setting in the sky.

Before they entered Robert's home, Robert pointed to George's cigar.

"Put that out. I don't allow smoking in my house."

The other man's face tightened up and he was set to argue, for no man told him what to do.

"You do want to stay inside, don't you? If not, you can stay in the shed," Robert said.

George frowned. He slowly put the cigar out. He placed it in his pocket and followed Robert inside. Robert smelled a delicious odor. Lena had set the table and had prepared supper. They all sat around the table and spoke of Lena's and George's travels and the things they had seen. Anna put her head upon the table after dinner and closed her eyes. Robert took pity on the child.

"There are two bedrooms upstairs. I don't use them. One has a tumble bed left from the previous owner who did not wish to take it on their journey west. Anna can sleep on it. Do you have bed clothing? I have no extra sheets."

"Yes, in the wagon. There is also a bed for us in it. I'll need your help with it." Lena disappeared to get her outer gear and followed Robert outside. He found it strange that George offered not to help.

Once outside, Robert spoke boldly to his sister. "What has happened to the farm?"

Lena turned white in the pale light.

"Tell me the truth so I can help."

Lena stammered, "George broke his arm two years ago. I did what I could to get by. We used credit until the stores would give us no more. George didn't pay the taxes on the farm, nor the payments. The bank took it from us. We are homeless."

She walked away, her head held high. She had always been a proud woman and a loyal one.

Robert never understood her attraction to George. He knew George could be witty and charming at times. It was no doubt that was the George that she defended. But he had a mean streak as dark as the devil himself that came out at times. Robert sadly shook his head. It would do no good for him to fight with his sister, for she was as stubborn as himself.

℘

Robert left the house early to go to work. Since the Allen house was finished, he was helping another carpenter build a house close to downtown. They had just finished putting up the frame and hoped to enclose it before the snow came. He arrived home tired but made a trip over to the Coopers' to explain the unexpected events that had transpired the night before. Emma took in all he said, and her face became quite sober.

"I'm afraid we will have to postpone the wedding for a month or two until my sister is settled."

Emma came over to his side and placed a hand on his shoulder. "You are a kind man. That's why I care for you. We have a lifetime to share together. Waiting a little longer will not matter."

Robert was pleased with her reaction but he had lingering doubts about his new situation. He had asked around town to see if anyone had an opening for employment, and he had discovered a few. He had a short list to give to George.

When Robert entered his house, he noticed immediately

many changes. Lena had put a tablecloth of blue on the kitchen table. There were two more worn chairs in the parlor. George was asleep on one of them. Anna had taken a book from his shelf and was reading. Lena greeted him with a hello, then promptly gave him a list of food supplies to get at the stores in town. Robert's mouth dropped open in surprise. It was obvious that his guests had been busy while he was gone and had now taken over his property.

EIGHTEEN

THE WAIT

Emma waited. The days dragged on and her spirits began to fall like the weather's temperature. The trees lost their colorful leaves, plants died, and the grass started to turn brown. One day snow fell, turning the world white. Still she waited, and slowly she became impatient. At first she had been glad to meet Robert's relatives. She could see that Lena resembled Robert. She had the same thick, dark hair, the square chin and full, small mouth. She was tall but not as tall as her brother. She was pleasant to Emma but kept her troubles to herself and did not seem to want to make a friend of Emma.

While Lena was quiet and polite, her husband, George, talked needlessly. He liked attention and thought his tales important. But after an hour of his talk, Emma blocked him out. What Emma liked the least was they seemed quite settled in Robert's house and made no plans to move. At first Emma felt sorry for their plight, but she became disgusted when a month later George still had not found work.

Emma complained to Mary, and Mary, good-natured as she

was, started to bicker with Emma. Charles noticed the arguments between them. Too many women in one household, he thought. He and his wife had talked between them of having Emma return to her parent's farm. When they had approached Emma about this possibility, Emma feared that would only make it worse and Lena and George would stay longer.

Charles finally found a solution. He took Emma to his law office two days a week and set her to work. Their clerk had moved on, and they were in need of someone to keep the accounting books and greet people while he and his partners were in court. Sometimes Charles sent her on errands in town or to the courthouse. Emma was quick at learning the job and found that she enjoyed the time away from the house. Charles paid her a small fee for her service, and Emma felt fulfilled for the first time. She had a new purpose in life. She copied the figures down neatly in a large book, and Charles praised her attention to detail.

One day when Charles and the other lawyers were away, a man with a long white beard, gray hair, and a walking cane came to call.

"Is this the Cooper's law office?" He seemed surprised to find Emma there. Most people were. All lawyers were men and to find a woman working in a law office was most unusual.

"It is. Mr. Cooper is at court. I can take your information and make an appointment if you wish."

Emma took out a book with dates in it. The man sat down.

"I own a business. I don't usually give credit, but one of my patrons talked me into it. He was a good talker and promised to pay me back. Now he refuses to pay and I need legal advice on what to do next."

Emma passed a piece of paper to the man.

"Put your name and business on the sheet." She then looked into the book. "Could you come back tomorrow at the same time? Mr. Cooper looks to be in then."

"I will." The man stood up. "I need to put a stop to that George Anderson before he does it to some other business. He has run up quite a bill. I don't even know where he is living."

"George Anderson," Emma repeated in horror as she watched the man leave.

That evening she confided what she had heard to Robert. Robert had had enough. He knew not how George occupied his time during the day. Lena said he went to town. George often came home late and stumbled into the house when the others had already gone to bed.

Robert became curious, and after Emma had confided with him about George's unpaid bill, he took a day off from work without anyone in his household knowing. Robert followed George around in town, never letting George see him.

What he found out made Robert angry. He dragged George out of the saloon. George put up little resistance, for he had drunk too much whiskey and could barely stand on his feet. Once home, Robert gave him a talking to. George paid no mind to Robert. Instead he yelled and screamed back at him. Lena stood nearby and had to separate the two men or they would have come to blows. Robert slept badly that night and while he stayed awake, he hatched a plan.

Several days later, George was in for a surprise. Robert had found him a job. He woke George at the break of dawn and told him to dress. He then loaded the man into his cart and drove his horse to the Simpson Livery Stable at the edge of town. George had a look of disbelieve on his face.

"Mr. Silver needs a stable hand. No experience required. I figured you were just the man for the job. If he likes you, you can continue working here. He will pay at the end of each week, but he is to pay *me* your wage, not you. I will keep part of it for your board and give the rest to Lena. It's time to pay for your keep, or I will toss your lazy hide out of my house and you can sleep in the street with the drunks."

George's face turned purple, and he protested as he got down off the wagon.

"My arm . . ." He held it out in front of him.

Robert raised his eyebrows. "There is nothing wrong with your arm. I've seen you raise it many a time, even though you pretend you can't."

Mr. Silver, dressed in dark pants and wool jacket, approached the pair and stood in next to them.

"This is the man I was telling you about, George Anderson." Robert pointed at George. With that introduction, Robert left.

George watched Robert and his wagon drive away. There was no way to get home, and he had no money to spend in town. He followed Mr. Silver into the barn and listened as he explained what he wanted George to do.

George found the work to his liking and from that day on he rode his horse to work. He had not worked hard labor for some time, and he was often out of breath. Mr. Silver did not seem to mind if he took small breaks during the day. George was good with the horses and had a wit about him that the customers enjoyed.

NINETEEN

THE ALLENS' PARTY

Emma stood before Terrace Hill's twelve-and-a-half-foot tall wood door that led to the entrance of the house. She felt like a dwarf besides its massive frame. She could not believe she was really here and would soon see for herself what all the commotion had been about concerning this great, new house. For weeks the townsfolk had talked about nothing else. When the invitations, estimated to be a thousand in number, had gone out, the lucky ones who had received them had gone into action. Women visited their dressmakers to have new dresses made. Men went to their barbers to get a haircut. The hotels filled up with out-of-town guests, and the rumors ran wild about what to expect at the celebration.

Mary and Charles had received an invitation, and when Robert received an invitation as well from the owner of the house, B.F. Allen, Robert had asked Emma to accompany him.

Terrace Hill was a three–story, red-brick mansion which spanned eighty feet across its width and depth. It had a three-dimensional Italianate style design with white brick trim on all three floors. White arches encircled all the tops of the windows, and some had balconies below them as well. A ninety-foot tower stretched high above the front door. Robert had told Emma one of the painters had fallen from the tower during the construction of the house and returned to work six days later. Tales like those had sparked the imagination of the townsfolk even more.

Robert pushed open one side of the two-sided door, which he told her weighed two hundred and fifty pounds. They walked into the vestibule, a small room that separated the entryway from the rest of the house. Emma was immediately awed by the woodwork in the room.

"Did you build this?" she whispered to Robert as she ran her hands over the smooth wood.

"I did," he replied.

Her eyes grew large, for the woodwork was beautifully done. He pushed open another wood door, and they entered into a world Emma had only dreamed about. Every corner of the house displayed the wealth, style, and taste of its owners, Benjamin and Arathusa Allen. Emma's senses became overwhelmed as her eyes darted here and there, trying to take in all the finery around them.

High above her were elaborate gas-burning chandeliers that lit up the house like the sun at midday. Piano music filled the air. She noticed three high arches spaced equally above the main hall that was fifteen feet wide and nearly fifteen feet high.

The ceilings were painted white and decorated with painted designs. Wood could be seen everywhere, on the floors, along the walls, and on the steps of the grand staircase. Their shoes made not a sound as they walked over the dull red Wilton carpet that was laid over part of the brightly polished walnut and oak floor.

To the left of the hallway, men and women had gathered in

the sitting room. They were engaged in spirited conversations. Their voices made a steady hum like a well-conducted orchestra.

Just ahead of them Emma could see the owners of the mansion standing near the drawing room greeting their guests. Robert and Emma waited in a line full of people to say a few words to their hosts before further exploring this beautiful house. Mr. Allen, a forty-year-old man of medium stature and a robust frame, smiled proudly at everyone that passed. His good nature and the heartiness of his manner seemed to please all that spoke to him.

His thirty-two-year-old wife stood by his side. Her fine figure was clothed in a rich black velvet dress with plain lace. Emma thought Mrs. Allen looked beautiful with her dark hair decked with roses. The lady entertained her guests with grace and dignity that Emma admired. If only someday she too could be such a cordial woman.

As they walked forward toward the couple, Emma caught a glimpse of herself in one of the two large mirrors in the hall. She wore the emerald-green dress that the dressmaker had made for her. Her attire was not as impressive as some of the other women who were clothed in fine silk dresses and with long trains.

For a moment, she felt underdressed. But then she looked more closely at the guests, and she found people from all different backgrounds dressed in their Sunday best. Some of the city's pioneers wore antique cuts of dress. They were indifferent to fashion trends, where other guests wore the finest styles from Paris. She need not be ashamed. Everyone was welcome there.

She had never seen a crowd this large in one home before. She felt like the whole town had been invited. Yet the house offered room in abundance and the guests roamed freely without the men blundering and stepping on the ladies' sweeping trains or each other.

Flowers were everywhere, casting a bright, gay, spring feeling to the event. Emma found this quite intriguing and wondered where the flowers had come from, since it was a cold, boisterous January night.

Finally, they made their way to the head of the reception line.

"Congratulations on your fifteenth wedding anniversary, sir."

Ben Allen eagerly shook hands with Emma's escort.

"Glad you could make it Robert, for this day is as much a triumph for you as it is for me." He turned to his wife. "This is one of the most talented craftsmen who helped to build our house. His attention to detail has made our home what it is today."

Arathusa said, "Thank you for your hard work. I am most pleased."

Robert seemed taken back by their praise and quickly introduced Emma to the couple.

"I hope you enjoy yourself, my dear," Ben said. They chatted for a few moments more, then walked into the drawing room. The room radiated warmth and was painted a rose pink. This room was filled with Grecian-style furniture consisting of two sofas, two armchairs, four sitting chairs, two crinoline chairs, and two French chairs whose cushions matched the wall. Emma had never seen so many chairs in one room.

Robert nodded his head at a gentleman and his wife sitting on one of them.

"That is Mr. Boyington, the architect who designed the house," he whispered to Emma. She turned her head to look.

"And over there is the Governor of Iowa, Mr. Merrill. I met him a time or two."

Emma was impressed that Robert knew many important people.

A heavyset woman of sixty with silver-gray hair pushed through the crowd. Her blue eyes twinkled as she came to a stop in front of them.

"It's so good to see you, Robert." She gave him a hug. "I was hoping you would return to my class. How is your handwriting?"

"Much better, Miss Jones. I have been practicing like you instructed me. You're one of the best things that could have happened to me."

Robert grinned at Emma. Emma was taken back by the appearance of Miss Jones to the point she could barely speak. Robert nudged her forward.

"My fiancée, Emma Edward."

"Hello dear. You're a lucky lady. Robert is such a fine person. I enjoyed having him in my class." She waved her hands before Emma could answer, and she went right on talking. "I was so pleased to receive an invitation to this party. Have you ever seen such elegance? The furniture was designed especially for this house by J. Ziegler and Company of New York. Arathusa's aunt, a friend of mine, told me a representative of the company came and oversaw the placement of the furniture. They did a fine job. Everything is perfect."

Miss Jones pulled Emma by the arm over to the pure, snowy-white mantel in the medallion style, with statues of Prayer and Water Nymph on top of it.

"All the mantels were made in Chicago and are very expensive, am I not right, Robert?"

"They were. I was here when the mantels were delivered from the Sherman Cole Company. You will find one in the parlors and library as well. I believe this one cost a thousand dollars and was on display in Chicago for a while. The Allens spared no an expense on the interiors and decorations of their home."

"The Allens are such nice people, pillars of the community," Miss Jones said. "Besides being a banker, he also helped organize the first gas company and the Des Moines Coal company. Can you imagine what it would have been like to have lit this house for the party with tallow candles and lard oil?"

"I cannot," Robert replied. "And we must not forget that he is also a stockholder in the railroads that run through our city and contributed to the Iowa Soldiers Orphans Home Association, an organization dear to my heart. He is quite a remarkable man."

"That he is," agreed Miss Jones. "Iowa's first millionaire, and to think he invited me, a nobody, to his party. Oh, there is Mrs. Carol Kenny. I must go speak to her."

Miss Jones stepped away from them and cornered a pretty brunette lady dressed in a buff alpaca dress with a long train. The woman stood in a circle of women near the drawing room's window draped with heavy, crimson satin curtains.

"That was Miss Jones, the writing teacher. The one you spoke of so fondly in your letters." Emma faced Robert with a complex look on her face. "I thought she was much younger."

Robert looked deeply into Emma's eyes. "Yes, that is Miss Jones. I grew quite attracted to her. She reminded me of my mother, who I hadn't seen for many years." He spoke softer so others didn't hear. "I hope you don't feel I tricked you into accepting my marriage proposal. I must admit, perhaps I didn't explain myself fully in my letter. I did take advantage of the opportunity to express my love to you. But I never meant to deceive you." He reached out and took Emma's hand and rubbed it gently. "Please say I am forgiven."

Emma could not deny Robert anything on this happy occasion. Although she was quite shocked that Miss Jones had turned out to be quite elderly, in her heart Emma felt everything had indeed turned out well.

"You are forgiven. I could never imagine my life without you in it." Emma smiled. "I can see now why you were taken with Miss Jones. She is quite friendly and outgoing."

"That she is." Robert squeezed Emma's hand and led her past the cabinet, inlaid with various kinds of wood, into the music room where a man, William Lehman, was playing on a Chickering Louis XIV grand piano with a masterful touch.

Kitty Allen, a thirteen-year-old girl surrounded by other children of her same age, walked towards them.

"Mr. Harding," she said sweetly. "I am about to sing, as are some of my father's friends, Miss Mate Newton, Major Studor, Thomas Hatton, and Joseph Sharman. Please, won't you take a chair and listen."

"I will, Kitty."

He helped Emma to find a seat while the performers were introduced one by one. Kitty wore a short pink dress, her skirt trimmed with flounces of the same material. She stood by the piano looking like a beautiful pink rose. When she opened her mouth to sing, her soprano voice filled the air. The young woman's voice was rich and cultivated, her poise even more so. She sang as if the huge audience concerned her not. Emma could have listened to her all night.

The other singers were just as good, and Emma felt like she was in a professional concert hall. The evening had exceeded all expectations that she had imagined.

After the performance, Mrs. James C. Savery came forward with a large box in her hands. She presented it to Mr. and Mrs. Allen.

"I know you asked for no presents to be brought to this happy occasion, but you deserve a house-warming gift."

Mrs. Allen open the box and found a complete set of glassware. She read the inscription on the glasses to the crowd.

"*Dieu vous gardé.* God keep you." She smiled broadly and gave Mrs. Savery a hug of thanks.

Emma and Robert rose from their chairs and walked out of the music room into another, smaller hallway that intersected with the main hallway. They found themselves at the foot of the grand staircase that led to the second floor. Emma looked up, and halfway up on the stairs was a landing where the stairs took a turn. Above the landing, a large window was situated, and snow could be seen falling against the black night.

"Would you like to see the second floor as well?" Robert asked Emma.

"Surely that is the Allens' private residence and they would not like visitors."

"They will not mind. There are some other things I would like to show you."

Robert held out his arm. Emma wrapped her hand around it and they mounted the stairs. Emma counted the steps as she went. Twenty, in all.

At the top, they walked into one of the four bedroom suites. Each room had a sitting room, a dressing room, and a bedroom. At the end of the suite was a door. Robert opened it and had Emma look in the water closet. The room had a toilet and a faucet for water and a bowl to catch it in. He turned on the faucet. Emma felt the water. Cold and hot water poured out. Never had she seen such convenience.

"You will have to build one of these rooms in our house when we marry. Whenever that will be." She giggled.

"Soon my dear. I think I have found Lena and George some lodging in town."

Emma trembled in excitement. "You are not teasing me, are you Robert?" She looked up at him, her face aglow.

"I am not."

She grabbed his hand and waltzed. He smiled at her pleasure.

"Come, there is more to show you."

They toured the upstairs, and Robert showed her a dumb-waiter that reached from the basement to the attic.

"The servants' quarters are on the third floor. The family rings bells to summon them when they are in need of their assistance. We will not go there, or to the basement where the kitchen, laundry area, and storerooms are located. But there are a couple more rooms to explore on the first floor. The family sitting room and a billiard room."

"Billiard room," Emma said. "I have never seen a billiard game, but I have heard that it just recently has become quite popular. The Allens have thought of everything."

They descended the stairs and ran into Emma's cousin Mary at the foot of them.

"There you are. You're just in time. They have announced that the food is being served."

Robert noted the time on a clock in the hall. Ten p.m. The night had gone quickly. The party had started at seven p.m.

John Wright, a caterer from Chicago, stood at the dining-room door directing the assembly of people to his creations. Ten minutes later, Emma got her first view of the impressive buffet.

In the center of the table was a huge flower bouquet. Plates of boned turkey smothered in port-colored jelly were at each end of the table. Between them were: three baskets of natural fruit, two Charlotte Russe fountains, two Nougat Pyramids trimmed with vintage grapes and oranges, two pyramids of wine jelly, two fruit cakes weighing twenty-five pounds each, a large basket of ice cream trimmed with iced fruits, one statuette of George Washington in lemon ice cream, one statue of a lion in vanilla ice cream, foreign nuts, oysters, comfits, confections, and other substantial items such as ham. To wash all the food down, drinks of lemonade, tea, coffee and chocolate were available, served in china cups.

Emma's eyes sparkled as she partook of the elaborate display of food. It tasted delightful. Never had she had such expensive fare. She would never forget this day.

The party went on late into the night, and Robert and Emma hated to leave, for never would they see again such a celebration.

TWENTY

THE INCIDENT

Emma snuggled her pillow and pulled the comforter around her. She was dreaming of Terrace Hill and all the finery she had seen. She wanted never to get up. Someone touched her face and said her name.

"Emma, awake up. Charles needs to talk to you. It can't wait."

Emma opened her eyes to the bright sun shining through her bedroom window. Mary stood impatiently at her bedside, a robe clothed over her nightdress.

"Get up," she said again. "Something terrible has happened."

One look at Mary's face, grim and white, was all Emma needed to toss the comforter aside and put her feet on the cold wood floor.

"Has something happened to Jack or Colette?" whispered Emma.

Mary shook her head. "They are fine. Here."

Mary grabbed Emma's day robe and handed it to her. Emma quickly put it on. She was quite puzzled as to what could be the matter.

Emma followed her cousin down the stairs. She found Charles sitting in the front parlor on one of the chairs. His hair was ruffled and he had not yet shaven. He wore just a shirt and a brown pair of pants. He looked quite unkempt. They had all returned from the party quite late, and they had arrived home in the wee hours of the morning. None of them had had much sleep. He motioned to the sofa.

"Please sit," he said. Emma did as she was told. He continued to speak in a soft voice. "The police came to our door just now."

Emma's eyes grew round as she stared at Charles.

"Has something happen to my parents?" she gasped.

Charles reached out a hand and touched her to reassure her. "They are fine. However, there seems to have been an unfortunate incident at Robert's house today. His brother-in-law has died and the police believe there has been foul play."

"Was he shot?" Emma asked.

"No, they believe he was poisoned," Charles said. "They won't know for sure until the tests come back. But by the symptoms he showed at his death, they feel that it is so. Dr. Brown had been fetched and was with him to the end."

Emma jumped to her feet. "I must go to Robert."

"No," Charles commanded, his voice loud and hard. "That would not be wise until this matter is settled and the murderer caught."

"Murderer."

Emma collapsed again upon the sofa, barely able to comprehend what Charles was saying. Mary sat down beside Emma and put her arm around her.

"It is not safe to go over there. You must wait."

Emma looked into Mary's eyes. They were filled with fear and sorrow.

"Promise me you won't go over there."

Emma could understand Charles' and Mary's concern and she nodded in response.

"How long must I wait?"

"Till the police find out who did it. They believe you might be able to help them sort things out."

"Me? Why me?"

Emma moved closer into Mary's embrace for comfort. Charles sat down on the other side of Emma.

"Because you know the family, and the rest of us know very little about Robert or his sister, or why this might have happened."

Emma stayed silent and tried to comprehend what Charles was saying. Thoughts rattled around in her brain, causing her much anxiety.

"Robert always kept to himself and didn't speak much to the neighbors," Charles said. "Whatever light you could possibly shed on this unfortunate incident would be of great service to the authorities. Dan Faner, who works for the Des Moines Police Department, will return shortly to speak to you. I sent him away so I could break the news to you. I felt if he told you what happened, it might alarm you too much. Please go and put on a dress and come back to the parlor when you are ready. Mary will do the same and I will also freshen up."

Mary squeezed Emma's hand and helped her to her feet. Emma had to admit that she felt shaken and was not sure her legs would hold her. With great effort she walked to the stairs and then up them. She was glad that the stairs had a fine banister to hold onto, for she was not sure she would have reached her room without clinging to it with her hands.

She changed her clothes in a daze and put on her stockings and shoes. She sat before the mirror on her dressing table and taking a brush, she combed the tangles out of her long hair, then twisted her hair into a coil. She pinned it to the top of her head. She washed her face with a cloth soaked with water from the bowl on the dressing table. The cool water helped her come out of her numb state.

She heard commotion from below and heard male voices talking. She assumed the policeman had returned. Out of habit she walked to the window and looked out. She stayed there a few minutes gazing out at the new-fallen snow coating the road and the lawns. She hoped that Robert would appear and give her his customary wave that would assure her that all was well. But he did not appear.

She took a breath, turned and went down the stairs to meet the policeman, but she did not know what she could say to help him in his quest for justice.

Charles saw Emma appear and quickly took her arm and guided her to the sofa. She passed the other man in the parlor. He was of average height and about the same age as Charles. The man was clothed in a dark blue wool coat and had a tall hat on his head. His eyes were dark and piercing. He did not smile, and his mustache hid much of his facial expression.

"Dan Faner, this is Emma Edward, Robert's fiancée," Charles said.

Dan raised an eyebrow at Charles's words, then took his hand and removed his hat, revealing a fine head of hair.

"I'm sorry to bother you, Miss, but anything you say could help me greatly in this matter."

Dan had a foreign accent, and Emma would later learn from Mary that he had been born in Germany and had just the year before joined the city's police force, which was made up of less than a dozen men. He did not sit down, and this caused a bit of uneasiness in Emma. He loomed above her like an eagle ready to pounce on its prey.

"Could you tell me how you met Robert and what kind of man he is?"

Emma nodded and briefly told of her romance with Robert.

"He is a hard worker, considerate, and has a sense of humor when you get to know him well. We expected to marry as soon as his sister and her family moved out of his house."

Dan's eyes never left Emma's face.

"He was also a soldier in the war," Mary interjected, "and some nights he prowls in the garden with a gun."

Emma frowned at her cousin with disgust. "He has nightmares about the war sometimes when he sleeps. Walking in the garden helps him to calm his fears." She glared at the policeman, daring him to dispute her words.

"I see," he said.

Emma could tell he was taking notes in his head of every word. His eyes never wavered from hers.

"Was there any disagreement between him and his sister's husband?"

Emma shook her head.

"None that I ever observed. I barely know his sister's husband. I ate dinner with them on two occasions at Robert's house. He and his wife were very cordial during the supper and their ten-year-old daughter was well behaved. But I have to admit I was a bit distracted during the meal. I had never been in Robert's house before and my attention was more focused on what I might add to its décor. I found it very sparsely furnished."

"Did you have any other dealing with his relatives?"

"Some," Emma admitted. "We all attended a comedy play at Turner's Hall one evening that stared Miss Blanche De Bar Booth. I had enjoyed my evening with them. Occasionally I would see his sister in the garden and speak to her, but then the weather grew too cold for such pleasantries."

Dan pressed her, further badgering her with questions about what she knew of the couple and if she ever heard arguments coming from the house between them or with Robert. Emma grew weary of his tone of voice and his accusations. She finally crossed her arms in front of her chest and declared, "I know nothing more that could be of interest to you."

Dan turned his head slightly.

"Do you know why they came to live with Robert and when they might leave?"

Emma sighed. "I do not. I know they came from Dubuque, Iowa, and had lived there for many years. Robert felt he owed them a place to stay, because he had travelled with them from Ohio to Iowa when he was young. He had lived with them for a couple of years. He told me last evening at the party that they were looking for a place of their own and it would not be long before we wed."

"Indeed." Dan took a step back from where Emma sat and turned his attention to Charles and Mary. "Have you anything else to add?"

Charles shook his head. "Nothing that I haven't already told you."

"Then I will be on my way. Thank you for your time, Miss. You have given me much to ponder." With that Dan hurried to the door and left as quickly as he had come.

TWENTY-ONE

THE FUNERAL

The funeral for George was held several days later. The weather decided to cooperate and sent them a sunny day that took the chill off the winter. Mary and Charles accompanied Emma to the service. They arrived just minutes before it was to start.

Emma walked to where Robert was and stood beside him. There was no time to talk or to tell him of her condolences. Instead, she grabbed his hand and held it. His face was stoic and unreadable. But he did squeeze her fingers, and the corners of his mouth turned up slightly at her kind gesture.

The service was short. A handful of people attended. Robert's brother-in-law had not lived long enough in Des Moines to make many friends. Robert's sister, Lena, stood on the other side of Robert, and her daughter, Anna, stood next to her. They looked as stoic as Robert, and neither of them shed a tear during the service.

Emma spied the policeman, Dan Faner, and she wondered why he was there. After the deceased was buried, Dan approached them and he tipped his hat at Emma.

"Robert, I need you to come with me. I am arresting you for the murder of George Wilson Anderson."

Emma gasped in horror and she threw herself into the arms of Robert. He held her solemnly for many minutes as the policeman stood waiting.

"There, there little one," he whispered to her. "I am not the first man to go to prison. Many of my comrades during the war also found themselves in such circumstances. I will be all right, and you will too."

He kissed her on the forehead and gently touched her cheek with his fingers. He reluctantly untangled her arms from around his body and nodded at Charles.

"Take good care of her. She is the joy of my life."

Mary stretched out her arms and pulled a sad Emma into them. Emma watched the policeman and Robert walk away. She feared she would never see him again.

Mary helped Emma into their carriage. So shocked was Emma, she could barely remember how she managed to get there. She cried into the handkerchief she had brought along. Her feelings were a jumble of emotions she could not name.

When they arrived back at the house, she walked like a toy wooden soldier up to her room. She tore off her coat and then searched her bags for the hidden items she had placed there. She returned to the front parlor and sat there for an hour, thinking, turning the items over and over in her hands. Mary and Charles, concerned for her well-being, came in and sat down next to her.

"I know this is a great shock to you," Charles said. "But I warned you not to get involved with Robert. Before you arrived, there was a horrible killing at a local bar. It was the talk of the town. Robert was in the midst of it. I know not what role he played in the incident, but in my opinion he should not have been there at all. This colored my opinion of him, and of course his strange behavior in his gardens did not sit well with me. I feared you were making a huge mistake by marrying him. But you seemed very much in love with him so I chose to look the other way instead of telling you about what I thought. Now I wish I had, and perhaps I could have spared you this heartbreak."

Emma raised her chin in defiance.

"I will not abandon him now," she said. "I believe he is a decent man and has need of our help in proving his innocence. I know nothing about the law, but you do. He will need a good attorney; one he can trust. I would like to secure your services for him."

"But you have not enough money, my dear, to obtain my service, and I do not wish to take on his case," Charles said firmly.

"I will talk to Robert and I know he has the money he was saving for our marriage. Until then . . ." Emma thrust the silver dollar she had found in the streets in Des Moines into Charles' hand, as well as the money he had paid her in the past few weeks.

"I am retaining your services. He is almost family after all, and family members should take care of each other."

Charles' mouth fell open with surprise and he tried to return the coins to Emma. But she would have none of it.

Mary watched the exchange and finally ended the dilemma.

"Charles, perhaps it would be best if you take on this man's case. Then no matter what the outcome, Emma can be reassured that everything was done that was possible in his behalf. Emma can have some peace."

Charles looked at his wife and thought long and hard about

what she had said before he answered. He did care for Emma and wanted the best for her.

"All right," he said at last, but he had little hope of winning such a case.

Emma rose to her feet. "You must take me to the jail so I can explain to Robert what I have done." She walked toward the entrance door.

"Jail is no place for a lady," Charles said. "I will go tomorrow and explain the situation."

Emma wanted to argue with Charles. How would Robert feel alone in a prison cell, believing the whole world had turned against him?

"Then I will write him a letter."

She sat down at the parlor table and taking a piece of paper and a quill, began to write.

TWENTY-TWO

THE MEETING

Charles walked into the courthouse, a place he knew well, but instead of going to the county auditor's or treasurer's office, he took the stairs down to the basement where the prisoners were kept. He didn't get far before he felt the damp and smelled the stench of the decomposing old hole. The jail's walls were made of soft-fired brick and stone. The place was dark and dreary.

He walked past the jailer's quarters. The jailer lived in the basement with the prisoners. Besides locking up the criminals, he also was their cook and their caretaker. The jailer, a man of medium height and stocky build, appeared. After a brief conversation with Charles, he led him to the cell where Robert was. Robert had a small cell to himself and had not been housed with the thirty other men that were there.

Robert caught sight of Charles strolling towards him and gave Charles a confused look. Charles' face was drawn and his mouth formed a straight line. Robert rose to his feet and walked closer to the bars of his cell. Charles came to a halt in front of him.

For a few minutes, the two men stared at each other. Robert was a man toughened by hard labor and it showed in his muscular arms and legs. Charles was as tall as Robert but slender. Robert broke the silence.

"Why are you here?"

"I have a letter for you from Emma."

Charles removed Emma's letter from his coat pocket. Robert watched his every move. His eyes turned suddenly sad and his mouth quivered. He placed his hands around the bars that held him prisoner. He clenched them tightly. Softly, he spoke.

"I don't blame her. All night I have thought of nothing else. How her name would be tarnished if linked to mine due to this situation I find myself in. I do not wish to see her hurt. I believe it is in her best interest to break our engagement, and I will not hold her to it, although it pains me greatly to say it. I want only the best for her, and this is not it. Please give her my best regards and tell her all is forgiven."

With those words said, Robert turned away without taking the letter that Charles held out to him. He wearily sat down on his bed. He placed his head in his hands to hide the tears that slid down his cheek.

Charles stood a few moments more in silence, pondering what he had just heard and seen. He did not know what to make of Robert. He knew not if he was guilty or innocent of the crime of murder, but in that instant he did come to believe that Robert did indeed love Emma and that he had put her welfare above his own. That was in itself an act of great bravery and selflessness. Not many men would have done so. This made Charles think more highly of the man.

"I'm afraid, Robert, Emma has other plans. You see, she has obtained my services to be your lawyer, and this letter explains our agreement."

Robert raised his head, and a shocked look crossed his face, as if he did not understand. He sat motionless.

"You do need a lawyer don't you?" Charles asked.

"I suppose I do," Robert said. His eyes sparkled in wonderment. "You'd do that for me?"

"Here it is in the letter. Emma has decided to stand beside you, and she has paid me a deposit for my service. Now come get the letter and then tell me if this arrangement suits you."

Robert rose to his feet and walked to the bars. He took the letter and tore it open carefully.

Charles watched Robert's face change from sadness to amazement as he read the letter. He looked up after he had finished it and nodded at Charles.

"I agree to the terms."

"In that case, we must get started," Charles said. He walked closer to the bars and spoke in a low tone of voice. "You must tell me what happened that night."

Robert put his lips close to Charles ear and told him his side of the events that happened the night of the murder.

❧

As Charles walked away from the jail an hour later, he barely saw the horses and carriages passing him. He was deep in his own thoughts. His mind was whirling around about how to help Robert. He had only to place a hint of doubt in the jury's mind to keep Robert from going to prison, and he believed he could do it. He had not defended any murderers in his law practice, but he always liked a good challenge. This could be the pinnacle of his career, and he was not going to fail.

Robert had given him a summary about what had happened after he had arrived home from the party. But Charles knew he needed more. He needed to know more about Robert's brother-in-law, George Anderson, and he knew just the person to help him. Emma would be able to help him get the information he needed.

TWENTY-THREE

THE TALK WITH LENA

Emma felt like a spy. Charles had told her to go over to Robert's house and talk to Lena, Robert's sister. He had even given her a suggestion for the start of the conversation.

"See if you can get her to talk about her husband and why they came to Des Moines in the first place. Any information could be helpful," he coached her.

Emma's heart was beating wildly in her chest when Lena answered the door of Robert's house. Lena's hair was braided in one long coil that fell down her back. She was dressed in black and her face was still as stone. Her eyes stared blankly at Emma.

"May I come in a moment?" Emma said. "I have some news from Robert."

Lena eyes flashed alive in a feeling Emma could not name, anger perhaps or curiosity. Lena nodded and led Emma into the parlor. She sat down on a chair. Emma sat across from her in the walnut rocking chair. She untied her bonnet and pulled it from her head. Her hands shook. Emma tried to hide her nervousness by quickly placing the bonnet in her lap. She gripped the hat tightly.

"This must be a very confusing time for you. Your husband is dead and your brother is accused of his murder. I can't imagine how you are feeling."

The other woman sat on a chair, straight and tall. She sighed, and her shoulders dropped a little. Emma continued, her voice soft.

"Robert has obtained the service of my cousin's husband, Charles, who is an attorney, to handle his affairs while he is in jail. Charles has visited with Robert and he does not want to put you in an even more difficult situation than you already find yourself. He wishes you to stay in his house as long as you want and to contact Charles if you need help."

Lena nodded. "It's the least he could do."

"If you need a friend, I am here for you. I know you don't know many people in town, having been here such a short time."

"I know some," Lena said. "My husband was working at the Simpson Livery Stables, and the owner and his other employee have been very kind. "

"I'm glad that they have comforted you."

Emma was running out of things to say. She rocked in the rocking chair wondering how she might convince Lena to talk.

Lena suddenly brightened.

"The people here are kinder than those in the town where we are from. When we fell on hard times there, they turned their backs on us. All they wanted was their money, and in the end they even took our farm to pay for our debts. We left in the middle of the night with what we could before they took even those things from us."

Emma's nodded her head in understanding. She hadn't expected anything like that.

"My parents own a farm and I know how hard that life can be, depending on the weather. A dry year can set you back."

Lena shook her head. "It was not weather that did us in. George drank us into poverty. He was a good man once, but he could not stay away from the whiskey. Everyone has his faults, even my brother."

Emma stopped rocking in her chair and blurted out, "Was he drinking the night he died?"

If he was, perhaps someone else had poisoned him. Emma could barely contain her excitement and tried not to show it. She leaned forward in her chair waiting for the answer.

"No, he was not. He had taken many people to the fine party you and Robert attended. He drove them in a carriage from the livery stable and waited for them so he could return them to town. He was cold when he returned home and drank only hot tea that Robert provided for him." Lena's demeanor changed. She became guarded again. "Thanks for coming by. I will show you to the door. I have things to do."

Emma stumbled to her feet. The conversation had not gone well, and she felt like a failure. What would Charles think of her? But on one hand Emma could not blame Lena for being reserved in her comments. Emma had never gotten along with the woman no matter how much she had tried. There had always been a barrier between them. Robert said that Lena thought Emma was too young for him and disapproved of his choice in a wife.

Emma followed Lena to the door and walked outside. In her haste to leave, Emma almost pushed Lena's daughter down to the ground. Emma grabbed the young girl to steady her.

"Anna forgive me! I did not see you standing on the porch."

Anna regained her footing and did not tumble down the porch stair.

"My father got sick and died. Uncle Robert has gone away. Do you know when he is coming back?" Anna asked.

Emma stood there a moment, holding the girl, trying to think of what to say. Obviously Lena had not told her daughter the whole painful truth. Emma could not blame her. Emma brushed the hair that had fallen in front of Anna's eyes back behind the child's ear. She dropped her hand as the girl continued to stare at her.

"I don't know when he is coming home. Soon I hope."

"Anna, did you feed the horses?" Lena's voice came from behind Emma.

"I did, Momma."

"Good, then come into the house and let Miss Edward pass."

Anna darted around Emma and went to her mother. Lena then closed the door behind them. Emma's boots made a crunching sound as she walked through the snow that covered the lawn's grass as she made her way toward her cousin Mary's house.

Anna's question had touched her deep in her soul. A fear overcame her suddenly, and she had to will back the tears that threatened to fall from her eyes. Would Robert ever come home? She realized for the first time how serious this situation really was. She had believed so strongly in Robert's innocence, she had not thought what might happen if the jury found Robert guilty. Charles had explained to Emma that if a person was convicted of murder, he would spend the rest of his life in prison. If that occurred, all her dreams and hopes for the future would never come true.

She banished the thought from her mind. Charles would have to win the trial.

Later that evening, after they had eaten dinner and Jack and Collette had been put to bed, Emma told Charles about her conversation with Lena. She apologized for having gotten such little information. Charles, however, listened closely to her words and did not seem upset at all with her poor showing. Instead, he took a couple of notes on a sheet of paper. He then suggested that Emma visit Simpson's Livery Stables tomorrow and see what the owner thought about George as an employee.

"I am well known in town," Charles explained. "If I ask many questions, there would be gossip, and that could hurt Robert's case."

Emma agreed to do as he desired. She would do anything to help Robert.

TWENTY-FOUR

HE HAD A COLD

The next day Charles took Emma to town. Mary had given her a list of items to purchase.

"You might as well do some shopping while you are there. Jack loves the drugstore, and be sure to bring him some candy," she said.

Emma had agreed. She also was told go to the bakery and buy some bread for dinner. She walked along Court Avenue and remembered when Robert had been with her. It had been a magical day. It was the day she realized how strong her feelings were for him. She missed him terribly and with determination, she walked quicker to the far edge of the business center where Simpson's Livery Stables stood.

The stable was a big establishment that housed some of the stagecoach's horses and rented others to town people. Some of their horses were for sale. In the corrals she saw some of the horses with their shaggy winter coats. One bay horse snorted and a white puff of air escaped from his nostrils. He turned his head to watch Emma as she passed. His ears stood straight up, alert to her passage.

Emma headed for the building that stood nearby and entered. A big man with a long, white beard and clothed in a thick, wool coat greeted her.

"I was just on my way out to attend to a sick horse. What can I do for you, Miss?"

Emma tried not to show her anxiety. She was not good at telling half-truths. Her mother and father had taught her strict morals, and honesty was one of them. But Charles had insisted she make up a story to gather information from the owner of the stable.

"I have a friend who will be visiting me soon, and she will have need of a horse to ride while she is here. I wonder if you would have a gentle mount for her. She does not ride often and is scared of horses."

The man studied Emma. She did not like the way he looked at her, as if he might devour her like a cat did a mouse.

"I'm sure we can find one suitable. I have one mare that is old but gentle. Anyone can ride her." He rattled off the cost for the mare. Emma nodded. She then licked her lips and went gamely on.

"I heard you lost a worker recently. My friend's husband will be looking for a job."

The man considered her request. "Have him come around. I might have something for him. Hopefully he will be a harder worker than Anderson was."

Emma wanted to keep the man talking. "Anderson, he was the one that died?"

"Murdered," the man corrected her. "At least he out of his misery."

"Misery?" Emma said, clearly puzzled.

"He was a good worker at first, until he got La Grippe a month or so ago. He wasn't worth a lick after that. He had a cough and was always drinking some concoction that the druggist on the corner on Walnut Street makes. Something called Smith's Golden Medical Syrup. One of my other employees, Harry, introduced him to it. He said it was helping him but I couldn't tell. I should have let him go a long time ago, but I felt sorry for him and his wife."

"He was sick?"

"Yes, Miss, he was," the man said impatiently. "Now I have things to do. When may I be expecting your friend?"

Emma stammered, "Soon. When he comes I will send him to you."

With that she walked out the door with the man close behind. She walked briskly down the road. She felt his presence and increased her pace. He soon turned and went to the corral where the horses were kept.

Anna had been right. Her father, George, had been sick. For the first time in days, Emma felt some hope. Perhaps Charles could convince the jury that George had died of natural causes and the attending doctor had been wrong. She almost skipped down the street, and when she arrived at Charles' office, she interrupted his work with her news.

Charles pushed back his chair and listened to Emma's excited chatter. He sat still for some time before saying anything.

"Yes," he finally said. "That might help, but we will have much work to do to see how sick he really was. I will talk to Robert and see what he remembers about George's illness. Good work, Emma. I think you have found a new skill. Perhaps you should join the police force."

Emma laughed out loud. "A woman on the police force. That will be the day. I can't imagine such a thing."

Charles laughed too at his own joke, but both felt some relief. At last they had some other explanation for George's death.

TWENTY-FIVE

JAIL

Robert sat on his bed in his jail cell. Life had been reduced to sleeping and eating. There was little for him to do except think, and he was not a man that liked to think too much.

During the day, time passed quickly as prisoners were shuffled to and from court. He found it interesting to see what became of his jail mates. Tim Bailey, a studious sort of man with a quick wit, had been jailed for keeping a saloon without a license. Robert had enjoyed speaking with him. Tim Bailey had spent barely a day confined.

Another man, Marshall Turner, was aggressive and angry. He had been caught assaulting a man and taking his shirt, and Marshall was held in jail with a bail of one hundred fifty dollars, awaiting trial.

Paul Rite, a young man of twenty, spent little time in jail and was declared a vagrant. He was ordered to leave the city.

Steve Wilson terrorized a farm couple just east of Des Moines at three o'clock in the morning and took their valuables. Steve was later found by the police in Des Moines and arrested. The couple came to town and identified Steve. Their belongings were returned to them. Steve was fined thirty-six dollars and spent several days in jail.

Fair and frail Lizzie Maine had been charged with keeping a house of questionable repute. She was fined twenty dollars and released. Robert was told this information by a prisoner who had been in the same courtroom with her.

Then there were the endless number of young men who were brought to the jail at night. They found themselves in jail for being drunk. Some had drunk so much they could barely walk, and when they talked they would slur their words. They smelled of strong whiskey, and sometimes they would laugh and scream. Other times they would sleep and their snoring would fill the cell rooms. Sometimes they sang at the top of their lungs. Robert was surprised by the crimes the other people did and vowed if he ever got out of jail, he would not commit any of them.

The nights were the worst. It was then that the walls of his confinement seemed to suffocate him and the odors of the jail overwhelmed him. He wished he could break the bars that prevented him from seeing the moon and the stars. He wanted to walk in his garden and feel the cool, night breeze, smell the trees and watch the sun come up. He missed his job working with wood and the exhaustion of hard labor.

He longed most of all to see Emma smile and hear her sweet voice. The dark night fueled his desperation, and the thoughts he held at bay during the day flooded his mind. He worried that he would live the rest of his life in this place. He now knew how his friends felt when they were captured during war time and taken to some even more horrible prison than the one he was in now.

He would stay awake as long as he could, but the darkness of the jail would lure him to sleep regardless of his best intentions. The ghosts would come and interrupt his sleep. Instead of just dreaming about military soldiers shot, bleeding and dying at his side, he would also see his brother-in-law among them, doubled up in spasms and in pain.

He rolled around on his cot, his heart beating at a rapid pace, sweat forming on his face and shoulders. He felt hot and miserable. His chest tightened with anxiety and panic. His eyes opened and still he would see their faces and their forms. He felt fear.

He jumped from his bed and paced his cell, lost in a dream. He could not escape. The images were real and alive as he relived the nightmare of his past. Sometimes he moaned aloud, but no one cared. His voice mixed with the others sounds in the jail. He paced his cell around and around, hoping to escape, but there was no escape, only stone walls and bricks. Finally, he would come to himself and remember where he was. He would despair and wonder how much more he could take. There was no end to his misery.

He sat down on his cot. He put his hands around his head and told himself to breathe slowly and to think of Emma. He would see her face, her sparkling eyes and calm, strong personality. Her image helped to steady his constitution, and gradually he would become quiet and find he could go on one more day. It was hard, so hard.

After several weeks of this dreary existence, a lean man with muscular arms was thrown in the cell with Robert.

"We are out of room," the jailer said. "Here's your new roommate."

Robert was glad for the new distraction and waited in silence for the man to speak. The two men sized each other up. The new arrival was as tall as Robert and about the same age. He was as slender as a pole rail. Wild, dirty-blond hair almost touched the stranger's shoulders and was badly in need of a trim. His dark brown eyes glared at Robert above his mustache and beard.

"What are you in for?"

Robert said quietly, "Murder."

The man blinked, but did not move. "Then I am in good company. I rob stagecoaches and train," he said simply. "I've been known to shoot a man."

Robert didn't flinch. He had served with many men who had shot other men, and if this newcomer meant to intimidate him, his words had no effect.

"Robert Harding." He reached out his hand. The other man grabbed it and shook it.

"Andrew Pitman."

They sat down on their cots and soon found themselves in deep conversation. Pitman liked to brag about his thievery and was a natural-born storyteller, exaggerating his adventures like a writer of a novel.

They discovered they had both been soldiers, although they had fought on different sides. Pitman hailed from the South and had fought with the Confederacy. He had lost much in the war. His family, farm, and friends, all had been destroyed. He had learned in the service to live by his wits and now took out his anger on the northern states by robbing for a living. They owed him, he figured.

Robert only shrugged. He too had seen the destruction of farms and homes of the South. He understood Pittman's rage, although he did not understand his behavior. War was an evil all unto itself. All who served were forever changed. Nobody in the United States had been spared. But the South had taken the worst of it, with many of the battles held on its lands.

That night it was Pitman who moaned and groaned in his sleep. He tossed and turned. When he called out in the dark, Robert went to him and laid a hand on his. The man woke up startled.

"You see ghosts too," Robert said. "They are not here, just me."

The two man stared at each other in the musty, dark dungeon.

"I fought at Shiloh," Pitman said. "I can't forget"

Robert stared back in wonder. "Me too. I was part of the Hornet's Nest. It haunts me still."

They spent the night chasing away the ghosts of the war as they retold the battle from their points of view. They recalled the sounds, the smells, those who ran away and those who died bravely. The feelings they felt during the battle spilled out of them. Their words could barely express what they had held deep within them for so long. But still the words came like the water flooding the land from a broken dam.

Neither cast judgement on the other. They had only been low-ranking soldiers just following orders as best they could. There was enough suffering from the battle for a hundred lifetimes. As the morning light shone through the cell window, they stopped talking, exhausted from no sleep. But the dark had passed.

"I've told nobody of the details of that day until today," said Pitman. "I have tried to bury the pain. I tried to spare those that have no knowledge of war, and men don't want to speak of hideous things."

Robert said, "A strong woman helped me share my pain, and with it I found some relief. I hope I did the same for you this night."

Pittman nodded and said no more.

"Andrew Pittman," came a whisper from the cell's window. A head of a man soon followed.

"Zach." Pittman rose and went to the sound.

Suddenly Robert heard a sharp clatter of something dropping to the ground. A pick with an iron head had been dropped from the window through the bars.

"I'll wait for you by Four Mile Creek next to the church." The man that belonged to the voice disappeared.

Pittman turned with a grin on his face. "Friend I have our way out."

He dropped to his knees and began to dig. Small rocks and dust soon sprayed off the jail wall as Pitman banged upon it with the pick. The sound was obscured by the drunken songs of their cell mates.

Robert watched in silence. Then he called out quietly, "The jailer is coming with breakfast."

Quick as a snake slithering in the grass, Andrew pulled his cot in front of his labor, tossed the pick beneath his bed coverings, and then sat upon it.

The jailer came, unlocked the door and set down the trays of food.

"I've been told your trial will be held soon," he said to Robert. "You won't have much longer to wait. Then you can go to prison or the hanging tree."

Robert grimaced. He took his tray and sat down to eat his meal. The jailer's words had pierced his heart. He had not thought of the future in many weeks. He had concentrated on just getting through each day, a trick he had learned in his military career. If he had thought of the future, the last bit of hope would have been drained from his soul and he would not be able to bear being in jail. Andrew watched Robert closely.

"I'd rather die running from the law then living in a prison. With luck I can dig my way out tonight. You're welcome to come with me."

Robert put a spoonful of stew into his mouth and chewed it. He would have to think upon it a while. He had always tried to do the honorable thing in life, but his life had taken a turn even he could not imagine. He thought about it all day long while other prisoners went to court and were released with fines.

Robert watched Andrew attack the cell wall with the pick after the light had faded and the sun had gone down. Robert listened to the pinging of the pick upon the wall. Prisoners in the next cell encouraged Andrew's labor. They kept up a melody of singing to hide the noise.

"Leave me your tool brother," one of the others sneered, "so I may be the next one to taste freedom."

Robert said not a word. He did not join in Andrew's flight, but neither did he discourage his labor. Robert liked the man.

The wall of soft-fired bricks was made of bad material and was no match for Andrew's determination. It gave way. The rocks and stones became bigger and landed in a heap beside Andrew.

"I think you have done this before," observed Robert.

Andrew laughed. "I have. Cell walls can't hold me. Where else do you think I got these muscles?"

The cell was pitch dark now, darker than the night outside. Andrew asked for no help. Robert got the feeling that the man felt a bit of pride at his undertaking. Robert could not see his room-mate anymore, but heard the cave-in when it came.

"I'm through," Andrew said, and he began to dig like a dog with his hands through the soil and the stones. The dust filled the air and made Robert sneeze. Andrew continued to work, and Robert heard him breathing hard.

After a long night, Robert saw the light of dawn burst suddenly through the hole. He watched as Andrew squeezed his lean frame through the small hole and heard him grunt as he pulled himself through the opening. Once outside he called to Robert.

"You're a bit heavier than me, but a little more work and you, too, could be free. Come with me?"

Robert was tempted to go, but he could not see himself forever on the run. He liked his home and had spent too many years working to buy it. And then there was Emma. How could he abandon Emma? As long as there was a slim hope to be with her someday, he would take it. He would take his chances in court. He waved Andrew on.

"You go. Good luck to you. Go quickly before the sun completely rises."

Andrew was dirty, with dust in his hair and smudges on his face. He shook his head.

"It's your funeral. Hopefully they won't hang you."

With that he dashed away over the lawn into the dawn's light, taking the pick with him to use another day no doubt. Robert watched him go and hoped he had not made a mistake. He went and laid upon his cot and stared at the ceiling. The singing had stopped and in fact the jail was quiet. Robert fell into a restless sleep.

When the jailer came later that morning, he was quite surprised to see the hole in the wall and even more surprised to see that Robert was still in his cell.

"He ran to Four Mile Creek. If you are quick, you might catch him there." But Robert doubted that the jailer would catch Pitman.

The man handed Robert his food. "You're a rare man," he said. "Why didn't you leave?"

"I don't like being hunted," Robert replied.

The jailer cocked his head. "I'll have Sam fix that hole by tonight. I'll tell the judge that I found you here." Then he left the cell.

TWENTY-SIX

LENA LEAVES

A loud thud sounded through the house. Emma rose and walked towards the door. The knocking continued as if the person was impatient. Emma opened the entranceway door and found Robert's sister, Lena, standing there. She stood draped in a dark gray winter coat, a red scarf wrapped around her neck and a matching hat upon her head. Her hair fell about her face as the wind blew a cold breeze around her. Lena looked serene, more relaxed than when Emma had last seen her. She held out her hand, opened it until her palm showed. Laying in her hand was a large key.

"I've come to give you this," she said. "I can no longer stand living in my brother's house. I am leaving and you must care for his dwelling."

Emma raised her eyebrows. "Where will you go?" She knew the widow had no other relatives in town.

Lena grabbed Emma's arm and placed the key into her hand.

"Mr. Harry Thomas has offered me a position." She turned her head slightly toward the wagon and horse on the road. "His mother has come down with consumption and is no longer able to tend her house. I will do the housekeeping and help the invalid."

"How do you know this man, and can you trust him?" Emma asked anxiously.

"He is a friend of my husband's. If it does not work out, I have come into a little money and will find another room," she said stubbornly.

Emma folded her fingers around the key. The metal was hard and cold.

"Robert won't like it. He will worry about you."

Lena tilted her head upward in defiance. "He should have thought about that before he killed my husband. He is no good, that one. You best be free of him yourself."

She turned and stepped off the porch, then turned back. "Be sure and feed Robert's horse. He will be expecting a meal this evening." With that she walked away.

Emma watched her go. A funny feeling rose in her stomach. Something wasn't right here. Lena climbed into the wagon and sat next to her daughter. The wagon loaded with their belongings was being driven by a man in a dark gray coat. He turned to look quickly at Lena, then glanced back at Emma. Emma recognized his face but could not remember where she had seen him. He whistled at the wagon horses, and they moved forward down the street.

Emma watched them until they disappeared from sight. She put on her coat and walked to Robert's house. She unlocked the door and went inside. The interior of the house was dim.

She walked about and noticed immediately that Lena had helped herself to some of Robert's furnishings. The walnut rocking chair that Emma had sat in was gone, as well as a chest. Robert had told her he had made these pieces himself. Emma had run her hands over the wood and had remarked on its fine structure.

Lena had also stripped Robert's bed of its bedding, and only the mattress remained. What else Lena had taken, Emma did not know. She had only been in the house a few times.

All the books from the bookcase had been thrown on the floor, as if Lena had been looking for something there. Some lay open. Others had their back bindings torn off. Robert must have owned a hundred books. Most of them told how to build houses and furniture. The pile of the books was high. Emma picked them up and put them back in their places.

Emma walked through the house and could tell it had not been cleaned in several weeks. The kitchen was filled with dirty dishes. The pantry held no food. Everything had been taken.

Anger filled Emma. How could Lena be so disrespectful to the home of the brother who had housed her these many months?

Muttering to herself, Emma set about cleaning up the mess. It took her several hours. No doubt her cousin would be worried about her since she had been gone so long.

Once everything was put back in order, Emma locked the house and walked back to check on Soldier, Robert's horse. He stood out in the small corral and nickered when she approached. It took Emma only a moment to discover that there were no oats in the barrel and little hay. Lena had taken everything she could.

Emma knew that Robert always kept supplies well stacked. He would not have left his horse in such a dire situation. Soldier pushed his head over the top of the fence and Emma rubbed his head. She would have to ask Charles to put Soldier with his own horse in his stable down the lane.

Soldier, a pretty bay horse, looked at Emma with sad eyes. Emma knew the horse had been used in the civil war. Robert had told her stories about his gallant service. He deserved better than what he had been given.

Emma walked to her cousin's house and waited for Charles to come home. She told him about Lena and how she said she had come into some money, which still puzzled her. Charles listened thoughtfully and said he would go tomorrow to the jail to tell Robert.

TWENTY-SEVEN

THE TRIAL

Emma walked with determination to the Polk County Court house, up the front steps and past the pillars. She entered through the front door. Charles had argued with her last night, telling her she should not sit in on Robert's trial. She had argued back.

"He needs to see me and know that there is someone on his side. Whatever the outcome, I need to hear what happened that day. I don't want the newspaper to color the event. I need to know the truth. I will not rest easy until I do. You have kept the details from me. You have not even told me a little bit about the case to ease my mind."

Charles told her that there might be some details she'd rather not hear, and it was no place for a woman. They were at a standstill in their debate, until Mary added her voice. For once she sided with Emma.

"If it was you, Charles, accused of a crime, I too would want to be there."

Charles frowned and shook his head at their logic. But he finally conceded to the women.

"If you must go, Emma, then go. But remember I warned you. You might not like what you hear."

Emma had worn her best dress, the same one she had worn to the Allens' fifteenth wedding anniversary party. It made her feel confident. She had taken a great deal of time with her hair, sweeping it up in a French roll that Mary had taught her how to do. But she felt anything but confident. She had come alone. Mary could not attend with her. She was staying home with the children.

Emma had ridden in with Charles, who said not a word to her, so deep in thought was he. They had arrived early, and Charles quickly disappeared inside the big building. She was left on her own to find the courtroom.

The first floor held many offices. The clerk's office, grand jury room, the auditor office, and the treasurer's office were all housed there. She found the stairway. She gripped its golden-colored railing and walked up many steps. The staircase was made of marble and was very wide. Four or five people could easily have climbed it at the same time. Upon reaching the second floor, she turned left as Charles had told her, found the courtroom and entered it.

The room was large, forty feet by thirty-seven feet, and the furniture in it was made of walnut. In the front portion of the courtroom was the raised judge's stand, the wooden stand where the witnesses would give their testimony, and the table where the lawyers and Robert would sit. To the left side of the judge's stand was a separate space where the jury would sit.

She looked around. The courtroom's ceiling was high above her head, and the room felt threatening to her. She made her way to the back of the room and took a seat on a wooden pew bench where the onlookers could view the proceedings. The only other person at the moment was a reporter from the State Register newspaper. She had meet him at the Allens' party. He nodded his head at her in greeting.

Soon other people arrived and took seats around her. The murder trial had caused much interest around town, and some of the town's folks had come to observe. But the courtroom was not completely full when the trial began.

She smiled at Robert when he entered the courtroom with Charles. Robert wore a sack suit, an informal men's suit with a lower collar and a jacket that hung just below his hips. He wore a vest and a plain shirt. It was the suit he had purchased for the Allens' event. Emma had found the suit in Robert's house and had given it to Charles so Robert could be properly attired for the trial.

The judge, jury and prosecutor entered the courtroom a few moments later.

The well-known prosecutor, a former probate judge and a former State Legislator, Jesse Dominic Johnson, took center stage and started the trial. Johnson had been a Colonel in the Civil War. His straight posture and the powerful voice demanded respect from everyone in the courtroom. He had been hailed by the local newspaper as one of the greatest criminal lawyers in the state of Iowa.

He was well into his senior years, but that only gave him a more distinguished appearance. His blue eyes twinkled as he stood up. He approached the judge, then turned to address the jury in his opening statement. The gaslights in the courthouse illuminated his bald head and the formal suit coat he wore.

"The defendant is accused of the crime of murder in the first degree." He paused after each sentence to let his words sink in. "It is claimed by the people of this State that on January 30, 1869, the

defendant did poison George Anderson and killed him with de-
liberation and premeditation."

He rambled on like an actor on the stage, illustrating his
words with dramatic hand gestures and the rising and falling of
his voice. Emma sat spellbound. She had never heard such a
speaker who could hold the attention of his audience. When his
performance ended he sat down, raised his eyebrows, and chal-
lenged Charles to do better.

Charles rose. He did not have the glowing credentials of his
opponent, nor did he have the long-distinguished law career to
bolster his argument. Charles looked outclassed, but he did not
show it. His opening was brief and to the point. After the long,
drawn out dramatic dialog of the prosecutor, his short opening
came as a relief.

"The state has made a mistake and I will show that they have
brought an innocent man to this hearing. The investigation ended
too soon and was incomplete. Who killed George Anderson is still
a mystery?"

With those words said, he sat down.

J.D. Johnson called his first witness, a local Des Moines phy-
sician, Dr. Brown, who was as round as he was tall. He had been
a surgeon during the Civil War. He had a friendly manner and
was well thought of by the townspeople. He cared for his patients
with compassion and generosity. If his poorer patients could not
could pay his fee in money, he was willing to take a chicken or
some eggs instead. He lived in a home not far from Charles and
Robert. Emma had often walked past his house during a stroll on
a warm spring day. He took his seat in the witness chair.

"Dr. Brown, were you summoned by a Mr. Thomas to the
home of Robert Harding on January 30?" the prosecutor asked.

"I was," the doctor replied.

"What was the nature of the call?'

"I arrived to find Mr. Harding kneeling over Mr. George Anderson, who had fallen out of his chair onto the parlor floor. Mr. Anderson was having muscle spasms of the head and neck which later spread though other parts of his body. Mr. Harding had his hand under Mr. Anderson's head and was wiping his head with a cold cloth. Mrs. Anderson stood nearby, crying for Mr. Harding to help her husband. She was also wringing her hands."

"What did you do next?"

"I thought perhaps Mr. Anderson had a seizure of some sort and went to examine him. Then with the help of Mr. Harding, we lifted the man off the parlor floor and laid him on a bed in a nearby bedroom. This slight stimulation caused him to convulse."

"Then what happened?"

"I was fairly certain at that time that Mr. Anderson had been poisoned, and I tried to administer some tannic to him, but he refused to take it. He then began to have convulsions with increasing intensity and frequency of the upper body. His muscles were in extreme contorted spasms that lasted ten to fifteen minutes each. His breathing was labored. About an hour later, he arched his back, with his head and feet the only things that stayed touching the bed. Death came soon after from asphyxiation caused by paralysis of the pathways that control the breathing.

"It was a painful way to die. Mr. Anderson was alert and knew what was happening to him to the end. His body then froze in the arched position and rigor mortis immediately set in. I knew then that strychnine poison was involved."

"How did Mr. Harding react?"

"His eyes went blank and he fled the room muttering, 'Run they're coming for us all.' I could tell he was breathing very rapidly. I could see his chest rising and falling. Mrs. Anderson was crying steadily and Mr. Thomas went to her and held her to comfort her. I put a blanket over the corpse, and then led the couple to another room. Once everyone seemed to have gotten over the shock, we talked about what to do next."

"Did you think Mr. Harding's reaction was strange?"

"I did, but you never know how a person will react to a violent death. I had no time to help Mr. Harding, for at that moment Mrs. Anderson's daughter, Anna, came down from her bedroom, and we all focused our attention on her. It is difficult to tell a child that her father has just died."

"Did you do anything else before you left?"

"I did. I looked closely around the house, knowing the police would ask me what I saw."

"And what did you see?"

"I noticed that there was a cup on the table, near where Mr. Anderson had been sitting. This image stayed in my head as I walked out the door. I then went to tell the police that I believed foul play had been afoot in the house. Police Officer Dan Faner went to investigate."

Emma sat back in her chair. She didn't realize how tense she had been at the doctor's report. What a horrible way to die! Mr. Anderson's death had been shocking. She could not imagine the pain and suffering. No wonder Charles had refused to tell her any details.

Charles asked the doctor a few more questions. Then Dr. Brown climbed down from the witness chair and left the court room.

Another man took his place on the witness stand. This one was very tall and quite old. He had gray, short hair and wore eyeglasses. He was slightly hunched over and walked with a slow gait. He carried with him a small wooden box and a bottle with a cap on it.

J.B. Johnson asked the man to state his name. The man introduced himself as Dr. James Brandt and said he headed up the Chemistry department of Rush Medical College in Chicago. He added that he was considered an expert in deaths caused by poison and had given evidence in three hundred other trials. He explained that he had examined the removed stomach of Mr. Anderson, which had been sent to him by the police shortly after the man had died, and that he had a small part of it with him today. He raised the bottle for all the court to see.

"What did you find in the stomach?" J.D. Johnson asked.

"After close analysis of the organ," Dr. James Brandt said, "I found a large amount of the poison strychnine, which came to about two-thirds of a grain in the stomach. Strychnine is a powerful, deadly poison used to kill rats and other rodents. It can be purchased for this purpose in any drug store. The poison has a strong, bitter taste. Strychnine has stimulant effects in very low does but causes convulsions at higher levels. A lethal dose to a human is one-third to one-half a grain."

Dr. Brandt raised the box from the floor where it had sat during his testimony. He reached inside the box and brought out a live frog.

Emma wondered why the doctor had brought the frog to court. The creature could be heard croaking. The people in the gallery stirred and leaned forward in their chairs to see what would happen next.

The doctor administered to the frog one-two hundred fiftieth of a grain of strychnine that had been taken out of the victim's stomach. The doctor then set the frog on the judge's table. The frog moved restlessly, but within two minutes it began to have spasms, became rigid and died. The gallery of people gasped. Emma put her hands over her eyes, no longer able to bear the sight.

Dr. Brandt explained in great detail about the spasms and convulsions that the poison caused and where the poison came from. Strychnine was produced from the Strychnos nux-vomica tree found in India and Southeast Asia. The poison was derived from the seeds in the trees' round, green and orange fruit. Most accidental poisonings happened when a person breathed in the powder or by the absorption through the skin.

J.D. Johnson looked up. He had been bent over at his desk, writing himself a note. He straightened up.

"In your opinion, Doctor, do you believe this was an accidental death?"

"No, sir. The amount of poison in the stomach was too much. I believe someone gave the deceased poison in a drink."

When it was Charles' turn to question the doctor, he got up and walked around in front of the witness box for several minutes, deep in thought, before he spoke. He then asked two questions.

"Could the amount of poison found in Mr. Anderson have accumulated over time?"

The doctor said, "It was possible, but not likely."

Charles tilted his head as if to ponder what the gentleman had said. He then asked, "Could George Anderson have died of some lingering illness?"

The doctor snorted in disgust. "No, sir, he died of poisoning." He emphasized the word poisoning.

Charles sat down and J.D. Johnson called his next witness.

TWENTY-EIGHT

LENA TESTIFIES

There were whispers among the people in the courtroom gallery when the next witness presented herself. It was the widow, Lena Anderson.

As she walked to the witness chair, her ankle–length, black dress skirt rustled. The dress accented her small waist, and her skin looked pale white next to it. Her long brown hair, Emma noticed, was braided in her customary one long braid that bounced upon her back. She sat down and clasped her hands together on her lap. She looked uncomfortable and nervous.

J.D. Johnson's voice softened, as if to calm the woman on the witness stand and not to frighten her. "Mrs. Anderson you were living with your family at your brother's house on January 30 of 1869."

"Yes," she agreed.

"How long had you resided there?"

"About five months."

"And during that time how would you describe the relationship between your husband, yourself and your brother."

Lena frowned, "There was some discord between us. Robert did not always like George's actions and was quick to correct him. Sometimes they argued."

"Can you give us an example?"

"Yes, when we first arrived, George had a hard time finding employment and he would go to a saloon and spend some time there. Robert disapproved."

"When you said he disapprove what did he do?"

"He went to the saloon and bought George home, he was angry and I heard his voice even though I was in the bedroom upstairs. He threatened to ask George to leave the house, if he ever found him drunk again."

J.D. paused and smiled at the widow. "Who was in the parlor with you that day in January?"

"My brother Robert had just returned from Mr. Allen's party and was telling me about it. My husband and Mr. Thomas arrived shortly after Robert and sat down with us. My husband and Mr. Thomas had driven many of the party goers in a carriage to the Allen house then returned them to town. Mr. Thomas had given George a ride home. They too had many tales about the events that happen that night."

"Then what happened?" Johnson smiled at Lena and encouraged her to continue.

"Robert told us he had talked to a man at the party that had two rooms to rent in town and he thought they would provide suitable lodging for us. My husband disagreed and wanted to continue to stay where we were. An argument with loud voices took place. Robert insisted that we leave at the end of the month."

Johnson spoke clearly and louder, "Why did your brother want you to leave?"

"Robert had proposed marriage to Emma Edward shortly before we had arrived," Lena looked straight at Emma when she said these words. Emma squirmed in her seat as if she had done something wrong. Several people in the gallery turned to stare at her as well. Lena continued, "He was anxious to marry and felt he had postponed the wedding long enough."

Emma was glad it was Lena who had to reveal the nature of Robert's and her relationship. J.D. Johnson had wanted Emma to testify but she refused. "I won't say a word," she had told him, "if you put me on the stand. I won't have Robert thinking I am against him in this." Johnson had not been happy with her. His eyes glared at her but she had stood him down glaring back at him until Mary suggested that Mr. Johnson leave her house.

"Go on,"

Lena tossed her head, "George got up from his chair and stood above Robert, telling him, Robert owed us some kindness since he had stayed with us two years when we had come to Iowa. He said we didn't have enough money saved up to leave. Robert then stood up from his chair. The two were inches from each other. I thought they would come to blows. George was still upset, yelling. He then started to cough and I took his arm pulled him back to his chair. I asked Robert to get something for George to drink. He went into the kitchen and I tried to calm George down. I could tell he was very mad for he was twitching with rage."

"Did George calm down?"

"He did. Robert came back into the room and gave George the tea. He said not a word while George drank it. Robert sat down and stared at George brooding. Mr. Thomas and I then kept up a lively conversation for several minutes." Suddenly Lena let out a loud cry like a newborn baby makes, her hands began to tremble as she bent and buried her face in them. Emma could hear her muffled sobbing in the courtroom. The crowd sat quietly, nobody moved in their seats, everyone was stunned by what they were watching.

J.D. Johnson rose from his chair behind the table where he had been sitting and walked to Lena, "Do you need a moment? I don't wish to distress you anymore than what is absolutely necessary, but you need to go on with your testimony."

Emma's heart went out to Lena and she wished she could run up and console her. It was painful watching the other woman sob. Lena sat that way for several minutes then rose up again after gaining her composure. Her eyes were red. Her voice soft. "George shook suddenly, he gasped and fell to the floor in spasms. It was horrible. I had never seen anyone is such pain. Robert ran to help him as did Mr. Thomas. Robert then asked Mr. Thomas to fetch the doctor. The spasms kept on for quite a while. They would stop then start up again. Then the doctor arrived. I felt helpless."

Lena began to weep. Tears trickled down her face. She took her handkerchief and wiped her eyes.

Emma heard the woman seated next to her start to cry with the widow. She also heard sounds of sniffling in the courtroom.

J.D. Johnson walked back to his chair.

"Did anyone else give your husband something to drink that day other than your brother?"

Lena seemed glad for the change of direction in her testimony. She seemed to gather herself to speak once again.

"No one. Just Robert. The doctor tried to give him something for the spasms but he refused to take it."

"Did you drink any of the tea?"

Lena shook her head. "Robert did not offer me any."

"Did you ever leave the parlor after Robert and your husband arrived?"

"No sir, not once. I was in the room the whole time."

Lena answered several more questions, then J.D. Johnson sat down. The crowd had been enthralled by the drama in the courtroom. Emma heard someone whisper behind her, "They got him now." Sadness overwhelmed her, and her hope was quickly disappearing.

Charles rose and paced back and forth in front of Lena several times. The gallery waited in anticipation. Finally, he spoke.

"You said your husband had a coughing fit. Was he sick?"

"No," Lena said firmly, as if she understood Charles' plan of defense. "He had La Grippe a month prior but had recovered and had gone back to work. However, he had a lingering cough. He had been taking a syrup for it to sooth his throat. But he was not sick enough to die."

Charles' mouth fell open. He paused, then quickly regained his composure.

"You said you did not have money enough to leave Robert's home, but that is not quite true, is it?"

Lena took a deep breath. Her mouth formed a straight line as if she was suddenly very angry.

"Robert told George that he had been saving the money we had given him for our keep and it was ours if we left. George didn't believe him and neither did I. It only made Robert madder."

Lena lifted her head and stared at Charles in defiance, her eyes cold as steel. Charles continued on.

"You stayed at Mr. Harding's house after he went to jail."

"I did for a while, but I am now working as Mr. Thomas's mother's housekeeper. I and my daughter live in her home."

"Before you left Robert's house, did you find the money Robert had saved for you?"

Lena's sat stone still. Anger crossed her face and she glared at Charles in silence, then said, "I did. It was hidden in the bookcase. I took it all. Robert owed me that much for my misery."

Charles nodded his head as if to agree with her. "Mr. Thomas has been very kind to you since the incident. Are you more than his friend?"

J.D. Johnson jumped up and declared that had nothing to do with the crime. The judge agreed. Charles smiled sheepishly and sat down.

TWENTY-NINE

DID HE OR DID HE NOT?

Emma sought a quiet place to eat her lunch during the trial's break. She found a large stone under a tree and sat down upon it. She unwrapped the sandwich that Mary had made for her. She was hungry but ate it slowly. She wished that she could have talked to Charles and perhaps he could explain to her what he was doing. It seemed that the prosecutor was getting the best of him. If this kept up, Robert would find himself forever in jail.

It was the first time Emma had ever even considered the idea, and she didn't like it. She banished the thought from her mind. Her mother had taught her not to worry about things she had no control over.

J.D. Johnson's gestures were overly-dramatic at times, and Emma noticed he played to the audience for effect. Emma admitted he was a clever lawyer and seemed to use every detail of the case to his advantage.

She looked around her to distract herself from her discouraging thoughts. She watched the people and wagons on the street.

He saw the State's Register reporter, who had been sitting close by her at the trial, walk briskly out of the courthouse and pass her without giving a look in her direction. No doubt in a hurry to write an article about the trial for the paper. Other people passed her, taking no notice of her.

The day was chilly, being early spring, and she gathered her coat closely around her. Another couple walked out of the courthouse hand-in-hand. Emma blinked her eyes twice and realized it was Lena and a man she didn't recognize. Lena was moving quickly on in her new life.

After the noon break, Mr. Thomas took the stand. Emma recognized him as the man that had been walking with Lena. He repeated much that was already known from the previous witnesses. He, too, declared that Robert had offered him no tea and he had only left the parlor to get the doctor. He stated that the argument between the two men had been very heated, and both men had been very angry.

Charles asked Mr. Thomas, since he had worked with Mr. Anderson, if Mr. Anderson had coughed much. Mr. Thomas shrugged his shoulders before he answered.

"A few times, but the syrup Mr. Anderson always carried with him had relieved his discomfort. I remember him drinking from the bottle a couple of times that day."

The rest of the afternoon, J.B. Johnson sent other witnesses to the stand. Some were neighbors that lived behind or next to Robert. They told of his strange behavior at night and some thought he was a bit insane and avoided him at all cost. One said he heard loud voices coming from the house early in the morning when he had walked by the house on his way to work. None of them said they knew Mr. Harding very well, or even what he did for a living. Mr. Harding liked to keep to himself. They did note that his house and his garden were well tended.

The last witness of the day was Dan Faner, the police officer who had talked to Emma. Some of the people watching the trial had left and few remained. It was getting late and the weather had turned overcast. Shadows had formed in the courtroom, giving it an eerie appearance.

J.D. Johnson however, seemed to brighten when Mr. Faner sat on the witness chair. The man had dressed very neatly for his in-court appearance, and his presence seemed to fill the room. A gleam appeared in Johnson's eyes or was it the fading light that had caught him just right wondered Emma.

"When did you go over to Mr. Harding's house?" Mr. Johnson asked.

"As soon as Doctor Brown summoned me."

"What did you do when you arrived?" J.D. Johnson drilled the police man with quick questions as if to raise the tension in the courtroom.

"I talked to all the people present in the house, telling them that because Mr. Anderson had died suddenly I needed to know what had happened. I talked to each of them privately away from each other. Their stories were pretty much the same, including Mr. Harding's. I then walked through the house observing everything."

"What did you find?"

"I found the deceased on the bed with a blanket over him, the house tidy with no signs that indicated there had been a struggle. The people were silent or sobbing. I also observed an empty tea cup in the parlor and a bottle of rat poison in the kitchen next to the stove not far from where Mr. Harding was sitting. The bottle said poison engraved upon on it so it was not hard to determine what it was. I took the poison with me along with the tea cup. I thought there was enough evidence to warrant Mr. Anderson's stomach being sent to the chemist. I sent the poison bottle along with the stomach."

"What did the report say about the poison bottle?" J.D. Johnson voice rose and he spoke loudly, as if encouraging the police officer to do the same.

"That the poison was strychnine and was most likely used to cause Mr. Anderson's death. The bottle was only half full."

J.D. Johnson had a wicked smile on his lips. "What did you conclude from this information?"

Mr. Faner leaned forward and had a sorrowful expression on his face. "I deduced that the only person who had access to the poison that day out of the people in the house was Mr. Harding. He was the only one who had gone to the kitchen. He was the only one who gave Mr. Anderson a drink. He was the only one with a motive and the opportunity to administer the poison to Mr. Anderson, so I arrested him for murder."

Emma let the words sink into her soul. She heard not anything else that was said. She had followed the prosecutor's logic, and she too could find no other explanation for George Anderson's death.

Charles rose and questioned the policeman, but to Emma he seemed to be doing it in a daze, so distracted was she. Had Robert fooled her? Had he wanted so much to marry her that he had killed another man? What kind of person was he? At that moment she questioned everything she knew about him. Had Charles been right all along, that Robert was indeed strange and dangerous?

THIRTY

EMMA TALKS TO ROBERT

When the court was over for the day, Emma walked through the darkened hallway of the courthouse and made her way toward the stairs that led to the jailhouse. Robert had disappeared down them just moments before. She knew what she had to do. She had to find out the truth for herself.

Robert had barely returned to his cell when he saw Emma walking through the jail corridor. Men from other cells made snide comments to her as she passed. She studied each cell looking for him. Robert smiled. She looked beautiful, and his pulsed raced with excitement.

Finally, she stood before him. It had been a long time since he had seen her. Four long months he had waited. Her weekly letters had given him joy in a joyless place. Just when he thought he could not take another day, one would arrive, and he took courage from them.

He took in her slim figure and her green dress. As usual, some of the strands of her long hair had become disconnected from her bun. He longed to touch the strands and wrap them around his finger.

The closer she got, the more Robert realized something was very wrong. The bright smile she usually had was gone. Her eyes looked sad and haunted. She put her hands around the bars of his cell. He put his over hers but she suddenly jerked away as if she could not stand him touching her.

"What is it Emma? Why are you perturbed?"

Emma frowned. "As you know I was in court today, I heard the testimony against you."

Robert's heart sunk and he could not breathe. "And you believe them?"

Emma shook her head. "I know not what to believe, Robert. Please be truthful. Do not lie to me. Did you kill that man?"

Robert stood stunned. He lost his ability to utter a word. Hope vanished. He grabbed the bars again to steady himself. He could not look into her eyes. He bowed his head and looked at the ground. It seemed to move under his feet, and he felt like he might faint. And still she waited with that same pained look on her face.

They stood that way for many minutes. He closed his eyes, trying to find the truth. Slowly he raised his head and sadly looked at her.

"I have killed many men during the war, Emma, but not that one. However, if fate decides that I should be punished for my past actions, then let it be, for I am guilty of causing other deaths, and I know it. If I must be in a cell for the rest of my life as the consequences for what I have done, so be it. It is a just sentence.

"But I would never want you to be sentenced with me. Live your life, Emma. Find what good you can in this world and do good deeds for others as you have done for me these long past months. I will gain much satisfaction from knowing that you are happy and well. You are a good woman, Emma, and a strong one. Tomorrow I will know what destiny has for me. I can only hope it will send me back to you."

Emma raised her hand and touched his face though the jail bars. Her fingers could barely rub his skin. She dropped her hands and squeezed his hands.

"I believe what you have told me. I have loved you, Robert, with all my heart. May it not break tomorrow." With that she turned and walked away.

The trip back to her cousin Mary's house seemed long. Charles, too, had been drained from the day's proceedings, and the only sound he made was a clucking noise to the carriage horse.

Emma broke the silence. "I don't think I will accompany you tomorrow but will wait at home."

Charles turned his head and studied her. "I told you, you might not like what you heard today. But tomorrow is my turn to present the other side."

"I don't think I can bear it," Emma said. "How could you possibly find testimony that will set him free? Even I have been convinced by the prosecutor that Robert is guilty."

Charles chuckled. "Emma, Emma, have faith. It is you who has gotten me into this mess, and I will get us out of it. You will see, for I have come to believe that Robert is indeed an innocent man, just as you always knew. I have gotten to know him better these past months, and I like what I have seen. I can understand why you were taken with him." Charles placed his arm around Emma and squeezed her shoulder. "Don't give up, Emma. Tomorrow is another day."

Emma ate little of the food Mary had prepared. When Charles started to tell Mary what had happened in court that day, Emma slipped away to her room and threw herself onto the bed. She prayed as tears fell from her eyes.

"I know not what tomorrow brings, so I only ask, dear Lord, that you protect Robert and let the truth be known. Let your will be done."

THIRTY-ONE

THE DEFENSE

Emma sat in the same wooden pew in the courtroom the next day. Charles had been cheerful when he drove them into town, but Emma could not rise to the occasion. She spoke little to him. She dreaded what was to come. As if to match her mood, she had worn a plain, dark-blue dress with no trim or lace. She let her hair hang loose about her shoulders. She had not the energy to bind it up that morning.

When the courtroom was filled with people, Charles called a James Smith to the witness stand. A thirty-some-year-old man with chestnut brown hair and a fair complexion walked to the stand. He moved like a deer, quiet and smooth. He sat down.

Charles' eyes gleamed and he seemed pleased with himself.

"Can you tell us what you do for a living?"

"I am a drug merchant and chemist. I own the shop on Walnut Street."

"Was Mr. George Anderson a customer of yours?"

"He was. In the month of January, he bought four bottles of Smith's Golden Medical Syrup. It is an excellent tonic for treatment of anemia, bronchitis, La Grippe, and wasting disease. My father and I patented the formula of syrup, and it is recognized in the medical community as an excellent recuperative tonic. I myself have used it, as have hundreds of other people. We have many letters of testimony from happy customers."

The man went on and on, as if he was selling his product to all those present. Emma could not imagine why Charles had called him to testify.

When the man had taken a breath, Charles took a piece of the newspaper and handed it to Mr. Smith.

"Is this your advertisement in the State Register?"

Smith nodded.

"Could you read to the court what the advertisement says about the ingredients that are in the Smith's Golden Medical Syrup?"

Smith pulled out his eyeglasses from his pocket and adjusted them on his nose. He held the paper up to eye level. He squinted. The print on the advertisement was blurred and small making it hard to read. "Let me see now. Smith's Golden Medical Syrup contains Benzoate of Soda, Lime, Potash, Iron, Manganese, Quinine, and strychnine."

Emma gasped as did the others in the courtroom. Murmurs were heard. J.D. Johnson moved uneasily in his chair. The judge asked for silence.

Smith looked startled not understanding what had just happened.

Charles spoke again, "tell me Mr. Smith why you would put strychnine in a cough syrup?"

"Strychnine has been used in medicine in low doses for some time as a stimulant and is also good for stomach problems. We put it in the syrup to help people feel less tired and gives them a feeling of buoyancy. A teaspoon of the syrup is to be taken at meal time. It's very safe."

Charles' mouth tightened, "Has anyone to your knowledge ever taken more than the prescribed dose?"

Smith looked confused, "I don't know what a customer does with the syrup after he leaves my shop. It really isn't my business." With that he took his glasses off and put them once more in his gray suit pocket.

Charles stared at Mr. Smith and sighed. "Perhaps it should be. Now Mr. Smith, when was the last time Mr. Anderson bought a bottle of . . . uh Smith's Golden Medical Syrup?"

James Smith knew the question was coming and looked at the note he had brought with him. "January 28, 1869. I remember that one because he came in with his daughter."

"And the date before that one?"

"January 23, 1869."

"How many bottles of syrup has he bought from in you total?"

The man looked down at his sheet of paper again. "Six bottles since December 1."

Charles looked over at J.D. Johnson. "No further questions."

Emma saw a glimmer of hope. Perhaps George Anderson had poisoned himself.

J.D. Johnson questioned Mr. Smith, "Have you ever heard of somebody dying from taking his medicine?"

James considered the question, "Not that I know of," he said. The man then stepped down from the witness stand.

☙

Emma was surprised when Charles called Anna Anderson to the stand. The ten-year-old girl looked scared as she walked to the chair. When she sat down her legs dangled, not touching the floor. The judge looked down from his higher stand and quietly asked the girl a few questions.

"Do you know what the truth means?"

Anna nodded. "My Momma taught me not to lie to her or Papa, and that is what truth is—not lying."

"You are in a court of law, Anna. You understand you must tell the truth today?"

The little girl's eyes opened wide. "Yes, sir."

Charles walked up to the girl. "Are you George and Lena Anderson's daughter?"

"Yes."

"On January 29th, what did you give your father before he went to drive people to the party?"

Anna whispered the answer.

The judge spoke. "You must speak up, dear. We cannot hear you."

Anna looked at the judge and then at Charles. Her brown eyes studied the two men.

"He wanted his medicine," she shouted. "It was in his room. I ran to get it for him." Everyone in the courtroom heard her and chuckled.

Charles smiled at Anna and tried not to laugh. "Just talk in your regular voice. You do not need to shout. You are doing fine. Did your father take his medicine with him?"

Anna nodded. "Yes."

Charles spoke quietly. "Was the bottle full?"

"Yes. We bought it the day before at the store. Papa bought me candy that same day."

Charles looked tenderly at the child. "Who told you that your father had died?"

"Momma and the doctor. The medicine didn't work."

"So what did you do?"

"After the doctor left, I found Papa's coat on a chair in the parlor. I looked to see if he had taken his medicine."

"Had he?"

"Yes, the bottle was empty. I took the bottle and hid it in my room. When Momma and I went to town the next day, I ran to Mr. Smith's store and I threw the bottle at him. I was mad. I hit him in the face. Mr. Smith tried to grab me, but I ran away."

"Was your mother with you?"

Anna shook her head. "No, she was in the store next door. She didn't know what I had done."

"How did I learn about your trip to town?"

"I was home at Uncle Robert's and you found me crying in the garden one day. I felt bad for hitting Mr. Smith with the bottle. You talked real nice to me that day and it made me feel better."

Emma's heart went out to the little girl. George had his faults, but Anna had loved him.

Charles sat down.

J.D. Johnson did not question Anna.

Charles had other witnesses. Mr. Silver told the jury he had seen George drink the syrup the day he died. He also said that George had been pale. The last witnesses were a doctor and a chemist from St. Louis, Missouri, who had analyzed the contents of the Golden Syrup. Both agreed that if Mr. Anderson had consumed the whole bottle that day, there was enough poison in it to have caused his death.

THIRTY-TWO

VERDICT

Emma paced in front of the courthouse near Charles' horse and carriage. Charles had made her wait outside while he went in to get Robert. Emma could barely believe that Robert was free. The jury had found him not guilty. For months her life seemed to have stood still. She could not move forward or backwards. Now everything was about to change.

When the two men walked out of the big stone building, Emma rushed to them and hugged them both with enthusiasm. She stood on her tip–toes, kissed Robert on the lips, and he kissed her back. He put his arms around her waist and held her close. They kissed a long time.

Robert lifted his head from hers. He stared into her sparkling eyes and a smile appeared on his face as wide as the Des Moines River was long. Emma smiled back and kissed him again.

Charles grabbed Emma by the shoulders and gently dislodged her from Robert's grasp.

"Emma, show some restraint. We are in public. People are looking at you."

Emma turned around, and indeed three older ladies were staring at her with shocked looks on their faces. Robert didn't seem to mind. He grabbed hold of Emma's hand and led her to the carriage.

"Never have I seen a day as beautiful as this," he said as he lifted her up into the buggy. He then took the seat next to her.

Indeed, nature seemed to share their good tidings. The sun shone brightly, there were no clouds in the blue sky, and the trees were trying to bud their green leaves. What grass could be seen around the courthouse was changing from winter brown to spring green.

Charles sat in the driver's seat. He whistled to the horse and they were soon trotting down Court Avenue.

Charles said turning to the happy couple, "You will dine with Mary and me this evening."

Robert's face beamed with pleasure. "I am most grateful for your hospitality. For I doubt that there is food fit to eat at my house since I have been gone many months."

Emma squeezed Robert's hand gently. "I did some shopping earlier this week in hopes you would be set free. I put some groceries in your house."

Robert groaned. "And do I have house to go back to. How are my finances?" he asked Charles.

"I paid the taxes on your house," Charles reassured Robert. "It was a good thing you had put that money in the bank instead of leaving it around the house. Lena helped herself to all the money you had saved in the bookcase. As for my bill, you can pay it in installments if you wish, once you start working again."

Robert sighed. "That is very kind. You have been most gracious to me, and I will be forever grateful."

"It was Emma. She taught me to believe in you."

Robert turned his head and looked at Emma, who was sitting next to him. He kissed her softly on the forehead.

"You are my guardian angel."

Emma sighed contently. "I am afraid you might find your house a bit changed. While I was waiting for the trial to begin, I spent some time with the dressmaker. When she wasn't busy making dresses, she taught me how to sew on her sewing machine. I had been hand-stitching a quilt, and she taught me how to sew the pieces together on the machine. I bought some fabric to match it and made curtains for the windows in your house. Nothing fancy. I needed something to do. Also, Charles put me to work at his law office doing paperwork and talking to customers when he was out. I owed Mary and him something for my keep."

"Emma, I have gotten used to you being there. If Robert agrees, after you are married I would very much like you to continue as my assistant. And if you like law, perhaps you could study to become a lawyer. You have a mind for it."

Emma blushed with pleasure. "My friend Bella from Mount Pleasant recently took the test to become a lawyer."

"I have heard she passed," Charles said. "She was the first woman to pass the test. Perhaps you could be the second."

"Perhaps," Emma said, but it was too much for her mind to think about. Right now all she could think about was Robert.

ॐ

The sun had set by the time Robert left Charles' house. They had eaten a fine dinner of roasted pork, applesauce, potatoes and biscuits. He had not had such a good meal for many months. Jail food had been slim and lacked flavor.

He had enjoyed his time with the Coopers. Even bashful Jack had warmed up to him and showed him his blocks. The trial had proved beneficial in one way. Charles and Robert had come to know and respect each other. Charles encouraged him to stay the night, but Robert had refused. He wanted to return home, home to where all this nightmare had started.

He carried a lantern that Mary had given him in his hand, the key to his house in his pocket. Before walking to his house, he took a short stroll down to Charles' stable.

He felt the cool night air touch his face. He looked up and saw a thousand shining stars and the full moon white against the black sky. He breathed deeply, filling his lungs with the cool air. He exhaled, then smiled. He could hardly believe that he was free. Free to do what he wanted. Free to dream. Free to marry and have a family. There were no longer walls and bars to prevent him from coming and going as he pleased.

He blinked the moisture from his eyes that had suddenly formed there. Never again would he take for granted the ordinary things in life, these gifts that all men were given freely by an unknown creator.

He heard a horse nicker. He walked faster. He came to the small corral outside the stable and there stood Soldier, waiting impatiently. The horse pawed the ground, then leaned heavily against the wooden fence, stretching out his head and neck as far as he could. The horse nickered again in greeting. Robert walked closer. He reached out his hand and rubbed the bay horse's forehead. Soldier butted Robert in the chest with his head in reply. Robert patted the horse's neck and ears and spoke softly to him.

"Good to see you too, big fella."

He stood there as minutes passed, enjoying the reunion with this noble horse. Soldier raised his head even with Robert's face and blew warm air out his nostrils.

"Yes, it is me," Robert said, and he smiled.

When Robert turned away, he could still feel the horse staring at him. He walked up the steps of his porch and pulled out the metal key. He placed it in the lock. He pushed open the door and stepped into his house. He walked around and noticed immediately the new curtains that Emma had made hanging above the kitchen window.

He walked to the parlor where it had all happened. He felt a tightening in his chest, but the room looked different in the dark and no ghosts appeared.

He lifted the lantern and walked to his bedroom. Upon his bed he saw the most beautiful quilt of colorful square patches. It brightened the room even in the dim light.

He put the lantern on the table near his bed and lowered the wick until the flame went out. He took off his boots and coat. He gently laid down. The width of the bed was wide, nothing like the cot he had in jail. He stretched his large frame out and rejoiced. He felt no fear. He smiled. He slept the whole night in peaceful slumber and awoke the morning to the sun pouring through the window. He quickly washed his face then walked out the door. He looked up into the second story window of the house next door and there stood Emma waiting for him to appear.

Robert waved.

THIRTY-THREE

EPILOGUE

Abby sat back in her chair. She had read a reference to Emma Edward in a newspaper article in the 1869 Mount Pleasant times. The article talked about the trial of Robert Harding, Emma's fiancée. The trial articles had captured Abby's attention. Emma had been easy to trace after that. In the Polk County marriage record Robert Harding and Emma Edward had married on June 23, 1869. In the Polk County census of 1880 they had two children a boy name Charles and a girl name Louise.

Emma's obituary had appeared in the Des Moines Register in 1926. It said Emma had been one of several pioneer female attorneys to practice in Polk County and she had been kind to all who sought her help. Abby wondered what had happened to Lena, Robert's sister. She discovered that Lena had married Mr. Thomas shortly after the trial was over and they lived together for many years.

Yes, Emma had sent Abby on quite a chase, but now Abby could add her to the list of her ancestors. And a fine ancestor Emma was.

HISTORICAL FOOTNOTES

Stagecoaches operated in Iowa starting in 1837 when the U.S. Office Department authorized a mail stage between Burlington, Iowa and St. Francis Ville, Missouri. The first stagecoach arrived at Ft. Des Moines, Iowa in 1849. In 1851 tri-weekly coaches ran from Fort Des Moines to Council Bluffs and returned. Twice weekly service began between Ft. Des Moines and Iowa City in 1852. In June 1870 the Western Stage Company ceased operation in Iowa after 16 years of service due to the construction of the railroads.

Des Moines, Iowa—The first building built between the Raccoon and Des Moines River in 1843 was a military fort. The area was opened to new settlers in 1845 and a year later Iowa gained statehood. Population at Fort Des Moines at that time was 127 residents. The city charter was adopted in 1857 and the word fort was removed from the town's name. The population of the town in 1860 was 3,965. Des Moines officially became the state's capital in 1857. The city continued to grow due to the expansion of the railroads which ran through it. Its population was 12,000 in 1869 the year this story took place and was a thriving trade center.

The impressive Iowa State Capitol building featuring a gold-gilded central dome and a classic Roman style, was completed in 1884, and it is situated east of the Des Moines River.

Today, Court Avenue is still an important street in the downtown area. It is often called the entertainment center and has many restaurants and bars located on it. During the summer months, the street is the location for the Farmer's Market. Thousands of people visit the market each Saturday morning.

The Polk County Courthouse in this story was torn down and a new four-story Courthouse was built in 1906 in the same location just off Court Avenue. The original columns and walls of the new courthouse were constructed in marble, and murals on the fourth floor were painted by Charles Cummings and Edwards Simmons. The 1906 Court house is still actively used by the judicial system and is the anchor of three buildings used by the court system. The other two buildings are directly across from it, one west and one north of the Courthouse. The jail is no longer located in the Courthouse but in a separate building north of the city.

Des Moines has become a national insurance and publishing center. It is home to several colleges and universities. In 2018, its population was 200,000.

The names of the businesses used in this story were found in the Des Moines City Directory of 1869. Most no longer exist.

Battle of Shiloh—The Civil War battle of Shiloh started at sunrise on April 6, 1862 and continued on until the next day. Confederate soldiers attacked General Grant's unsuspecting Union army of 40,000 men who were camping near Pittsburg Landing, a steamboat dock on the Tennessee River. The battle was named after the small Methodist chapel named Shiloh, meaning the Place of Peace, which was located on the battlefield. All morning the Confederate army drove the Union army northward, leaving mutilated bodies of men from both sides on the grounds. By midday, the Union soldiers had retreated to a forest which was bisected by a wagon trail called the Sunken Road. Here the Union soldiers made their stand. This area was later referred to as the Hornet's Nest. The Hornet's Nest collapsed around six p.m. and it looked like the Union army would be defeated.

Near sundown, the second Union army under the direction of General Don Buell arrived. Grant then placed a battery of siege guns on the union line and their fire drove the Confederates back. By two p.m. on April 7, the south withdrew. Eleven military units from Iowa (including 2nd, 3rd, 6th, 7th, 8th, 11th, 12th, 14th, 15th, and 16th) made up of 6,664 men fought in the battle of Shiloh. Many of these regiments formed the heart of the Hornet Nest. Two thousand four hundred nine Iowa soldiers were killed, wounded, or declared missing after the battle was over. Some were taken prisoners.

A monument dedicated to the Iowa soldiers was built on the Shiloh battlefield in 1906. Three thousand five hundred eight men (from both sides) were killed and another 16,000 wounded during the battle.

A total of 650,000 American soldiers died in the Civil War.

Sewing Machines—were patented in the USA in 1846. It was the first complex household appliance to find a national market. In 1867, Godey's Lady's Book said it took a woman an average of 20,620 hand stitches to make a shirt. A competent seamstress could complete the shirt in about ten to fourteen hours. The same shirt could be made with a sewing machine in about an hour. In 1862, three out of four new sewing machines were purchased by garment manufacturers. Readymade clothing was mostly work clothes of poor quality. Smaller, lighter machines were soon designed in fine wood cabinets and were sold to housewives on a monthly installment plan of three to five dollars. For women who made clothes for their families, the sewing machine cut down on the time to make the garments.

My grandmother, who was born in 1889, had a treadle sewing machine (you had to push a pedal with your foot underneath the sewing machine to make the needle go up and down). She was a wonderful seamstress and made many dresses for her granddaughters (me and my sisters) during the time she was alive. She also made quilts. She made one for me when she was ninety. I inherited her sewing machine when she died, and I still have it and the quilt she made me.

Terrace Hill Mansion—was built by Iowa's first millionaire, Benjamin F. Allen.

A few years after the party, Allen lost his fortune and Terrace Hill was sold to Frederick M. Hubbell, a prominent Des Moines business man. In 1971 the Hubbell family donated the mansion to the State of Iowa to be used as the Governor's residence. The mansion's first two floors have been restored to their original 1870 condition and are decorated with furniture and art work of that time period. The Iowa Governor and family live on the modern third floor. Terrace Hill is designated as a National Historic Landmark and is open to the public for tours.

Blanche De Bar Booth (1844–1925) was the niece of John Wilkes Booth, who killed President Abraham Lincoln. She was an actress and made her stage debut in 1865 in St. Louis, Missouri. She toured the West and the South starring in theater roles. She did perform in Des Moines at the Turner's Hall in a first–class, elegant comedy.

Adam Hafner was a real police officer in Des Moines, Iowa. My police officer, Dan Faner, is based on him. Hafner joined the police force in 1869, the year the Des Moines Department was first established. He was born in Germany and arrived in the United States with his family in 1854. After doing a number of different jobs in several different states, he settled in Des Moines in 1860. In 1874, Hafner was elected to the job of city marshal at time when the city was going through a major crime epidemic. Much of the crime happened near the police station that was located on 3rd and Court.

Faner's role in my story is total fiction, as is the story's murder. The first murder in Des Moines judicial record happened in 1854, when Pleasant Fouts was indicted for the murder of his wife. He was convicted and spent the rest of his life in prison.

The State Register reported that on March 3, 1869, there was a stabbing at the Gottgchalk's Saloon located on Third and Court. William Christ and Frank Rudge were stabbed in the breast and stomach. Two doctors were called to help the wounded. Rudge died but Christ lived. Mart McHerry and Mike McDonnell were arrested for the murder. On May 24, a news article in the same paper wrote that William Christ had recovered from his injuries and was seeking employment to work off his medical bills. William had been a drummer during the Civil War.

The poison strychnine was used in medical syrups in the 1870s and in early 1900, including one called Fellows Syrup of Hypophoshites, which was said to cure people that had anemia, bronchitis, influenza, and tuberculosis. It is listed in many medical books of the time as an excellent recuperative tonic. It was patented and internationally recognized by James Fellow, who worked with his father as a drug merchant in Canada. Its listed ingredients are quinine, strychnine, iron, lime, potash, phosphorus and manganese.

Arabella Mansfield became the first female lawyer in the United States in 1869. She was admitted to the Iowa bar. Iowa was the first state in the union to admit women to the practice of law. Arabella (prior to becoming a lawyer) studied at Iowa Wesleyan College in Mount Pleasant, Iowa in 1862 and graduated in three years as valedictorian.

The Polk County Poor House was constructed in May 1865 as a remedy to house the increasing poor found in Polk County. The Polk County Poor House consisted of fifty acres of land and a frame house two stories high. It was located north of Des Moines on what is now US Highway 69, also known as NE Fourteenth Street. The Poor House was closed in 1972 and torn down. The Polk County Sheriff Department Building now occupies this land.

ABOUT THE AUTHOR

P.J. Hick is a graduate of the University of Iowa. She is the past President of the Iowa Writers' Corner organization. She has worked in the Justice system for thirty years. She is also the author of two other mystery novels, *Vision* and *Dodge*.